# Contents

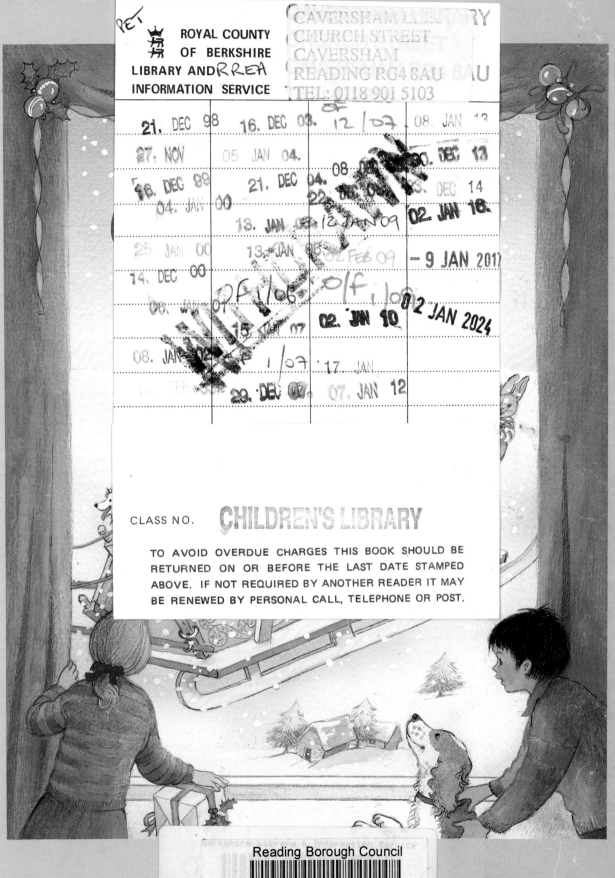

*Other Anthologies edited by Dennis Pepper*

An Oxford Book of Christmas Stories
The Oxford Book of Scarytales
The Oxford Book of Animal Stories
The Oxford Funny Story Book
The Young Oxford Book of Ghost Stories
The Young Oxford Book of Supernatural Stories
The Young Oxford Book of Nasty Endings

Oxford University Press, Great Clarendon Street, Oxford OX2 6DP

*Oxford New York*
*Athens Auckland Bangkok Bogota Bombay*
*Buenos Aires Calcutta Cape Town Dar es Salaam*
*Delhi Florence Hong Kong Istanbul Karachi*
*Kuala Lumpur Madras Madrid Melbourne*
*Mexico City Nairobi Paris Singapore*
*Taipei Tokyo Toronto Warsaw*

and associated companies in
*Berlin Ibadan*

*Oxford* is a trade mark of Oxford University Press

This selection and arrangement © Dennis Pepper 1990
First published 1990
First published in paperback 1993
Reprinted in paperback with new cover 1997

British Library Cataloguing in Publication Data
Pepper, Dennis
Oxford Christmas storybook
1. Children's literature in English, 1945–Anthologies
I. Title
820.8'09282

ISBN 0–19–278136–7

Printed in Hong Kong

# The Robin and the Christmas Tree

A Scottish Traveller Story

DUNCAN WILLIAMSON

It was around Christmas time when a little robin was hopping through the forest, and some boys who were out playing saw the little bird. Robins are very friendly. Wherever you are in the forest they'll always come up to you. And one of the boys who was a wee bit wild and vicious said, 'There's a robin!' He picked up a stone, threw it and hit the little robin. It went fluttering away among the grass. The boys walked on, never giving it a thought.

So the little robin crawled out from under the grass. He knew he wouldn't be able to fly for many months to come, because his wing was broken. And it being the cold winter time he thought to himself, 'I'll have to find shelter, a place where I can sit and rest and find some food, where nothing can touch me.' He lived in the forest where there were many many trees of all description: ash, willow, beech, oak, fir, and all kinds of trees. So the robin's first thought was, 'I must go and

12

ask one of the trees to give me shelter because I can't go to humans—they'll just break my other wing.'

He pulled his little broken wing, trailed it behind him and hopped through the forest. The first tree he came to was a large beech and he said, 'Please, Mister Beech Tree, please help me!'

And the beech tree spoke to the robin, 'What do you want, little bird?'

He said, 'Some wicked boys have broken my wing, and I need shelter. I wonder, could you help me? Could you let me shelter in your branches for a while till my wing heals?'

'Be off with you, be on your way!' said the beech tree. 'I've no time for you little birds. You come here, you pick my nuts and eat my seeds. Be on your way, I've no time for you!'

And the poor bird hopped further through the forest. It started to snow. He hopped on, dragging his broken wing, and he came to a large oak tree. The oak had many branches and many hollows, crooks and turns in which the robin could have found shelter. 'Please, Mister Oak Tree, would you help me?' said the little robin.

'What do you want?' said the oak tree.

He said, 'Some evil boys have broken my wing and I need shelter. Would you please let me sleep in some of your branches till my wing heals?'

'Be on your way!' said the oak tree. 'I have no time for you little pests. You pick my acorns and eat all my seeds, sit on my leaves and whistle all day long. You are just a nuisance—be on your way!'

So the poor little robin hopped further on through

the forest among the snow till he came to a fir tree, a larch. 'Please, Mister Fir Tree,' he said, 'help me! Please!'

'What do you want?' said the larch.

'I need shelter for the winter-time,' said the little robin. 'Some boys have broken my wing and I can't fly. And I wonder if you could let me sit in your branches for a while till my wing rests and heals itself?'

'Be on your way!' said the fir tree. 'I've no time for you little birds. You sit and you chirp, you pick my needles off and hop among my branches disturbing my cones and eating my seeds. Be on your way!'

The little robin couldn't find shelter anywhere. So he hopped on further and he came to a large ash tree. 'Please, Mister Ash Tree,' the robin said, 'help me,

please! I'm just a poor little robin with a broken wing and I need shelter.'

'Be on your way!' said the ash tree. 'You little chirping creatures—I have no time for you. I know what you do: you eat my seeds, you sit and chirp, sing all summer and when the winter comes you don't do anything for yourselves, but seek to find shelter with us. Be on your way!'

The poor robin hopped on its way among the snow, dragging its wing. It knew in its own mind no one was going to give it shelter. At last it came to a small fir tree, a little spruce. And the spruce grows very tight in its branches, where it's warm. The robin hopped up to the little tree and said, 'Please, little Spruce, would you help me?'

And the spruce said, 'What's the trouble, little bird?'

He said, 'Some evil boys threw stones at me and I think my wing is broken. I've asked all the trees in the forest for shelter and no one will give me any help.'

'Is that true?' said the spruce tree.

'Yes, it's true,' said the little bird. 'They ordered me on my way.'

'Come, come,' said the spruce tree, 'that's not the way to treat a little bird. Little birds should be treated more respectfully than that. I have many branches in my tree which are fine and warm, and many seeds have fallen which will never reach the ground and will never grow. Hop up on my branches, little bird,' she said. 'Cuddle in my heart and you'll find warmth. I will whisper in the wind and sing you beautiful songs.' And the spruce lowered one of her branches down. The little bird hopped up and he crawled away into the centre of the little tree. He was warm and comfortable and there were plenty of seeds lying around which had fallen from the top of the tree.

But he didn't know—a woodland fairy had stopped to rest on the same little spruce tree on her way back to the forest. She heard the conversation between the tree and the little bird. And she said, 'Those wicked trees!' She heard the robin telling the story, how the trees had ordered it on and wouldn't help it. 'Those wicked trees'll have to suffer for what they did to this little bird. But not you, my little friend,' she said to the spruce tree, 'not you.'

Then she flew on her way to the middle of the forest, and who did she meet but the North Wind. The North Wind was one of her greatest friends. So were the East Wind and the West Wind and the South Wind. She told the North Wind the same story I'm telling you.

And the North Wind said, 'Terrible, terrible! Terrible that these trees would do that to such a little bird. But,' he said, 'they will suffer, I will see to it. Oh, they'll suffer! They'll be cold in the winter when I blow through the forest. I'll blow every leaf and every twig off them, every rotten twig and leaf the next time I pass through the forest. And they'll need shelter! But the little spruce tree I will leave alone. And her branches will be green the whole year round and beautiful. She'll be the pride of the forest. Everyone'll love her.'

And lo and behold, the next time the North Wind blew through the forest, he blew every single leaf off the ash tree, the oak tree, the beech tree, and every needle off the larch—left them naked. But the little tree, the spruce, he never touched. He passed on softly, held his breath when he passed her by. And for all year round after that the spruce tree was green and beautiful.

The little robin sat there all winter through. His wing healed and got better. He lived on the seeds that

18

fell from the little tree. And in the summer time he flew away to find a mate, make a nest and have little birds. But always in the winter time he flew back and perched on the top of the little tree. Before he settled down for the winter he sat there, whistled and sang to his heart's content, because the little spruce loved to hear the robin singing his beautiful songs.

So that's why till this day, when people celebrate Christmas in their house, they always love to have a little robin on their tree. And that is the story of the Christmas tree and the robin.

# *The Rebellious Plum Pudding*

GERALDINE McCAUGHREAN

Can you imagine how it would be if Christmas weren't allowed? If it were against the law? If you were put in prison for saying, 'Happy Christmas!'

There was such a time.* Gloomy men dressed in black ruled the country without smiling, and Christmas itself was made an outlaw. No services at church. No holidays from work. No feasts or parties. And the town-crier shook his handbell and went through the streets shouting, 'No Christ-mass! No Christ-massing! No Christ-mass by order of the Law!'

Soldiers went from house to house, searching for disobedient Christmassers. A fat goose plucked and ready for cooking, a sprig of holly decorating the fireplace, the sound of carol-singing—they were all of them reason enough for the soldiers to break down the door and drag a family away to prison.

* In 1647 Oliver Cromwell really did ban Christmas. There were riots in the streets and many people were put in prison for defying the Government and the soldiers and celebrating Christmas as they had always done.

As you can imagine, the prisons were *very* full. A lot of people absolutely refused to do without Christmas. They hid their goose in the loft, they sang their carols in the fields and woods or in soft voices when no one was near, and they whispered to their neighbours through the walls: 'A merry Christmas to you, neighbour!'

But there was one thing that was extremely hard to hide, and that was the smell of plum pudding cooking. Christmas isn't Christmas without a plum pudding. But a pudding takes a long, long time to cook, and there is no keeping that lovely steam under the lid of the pan. So:

'What's that delicious smell creeping between Mrs Baker's shutters? Plum pudding! Away with her to prison!'

'What's that delectable smell curling out of the smithy's stable? Plum pudding! Clap him in gaol!'

That's why, when soldiers turned into Market Lane with a crunch-crunch of boots in the snow, Mr Tinker said to his children, 'Quick! Quick! We must hide the pudding! The pudding must be got rid of!'

It was hot, hot, hot. They burnt their fingers getting it out of the pan. They tossed it from one to another: 'Ow, ow! It's hot! Take it!'

'Ow, ow! Here, catch!'

'Hide it! Hide it quick! *Hide the pudding!*'

A rattle at the latch and in burst a Sergeant as big as

the giant in the story who could smell the blood of Englishmen: 'Fee! Fie! I smell plum pudding!' he roared. 'I smell *Christmassing*!'

But the Tinkers only blinked at him, all licking their fingers. And they said, 'Plum pudding? Surely not!' as the snow blew in through the open window in little flurries. The Sergeant searched the house from top to bottom, and he smelled that smell in every nook and

cranny, till his nose twitched and his mouth watered. But he could not find a pudding.

Meanwhile, out in the garden next-door, a little boy was building a snowman, a Christmas snowman, when the Tinker's plum pudding came flying out of the window. 'That's just right for the head,' he said when the pudding came rolling by, all coated in snow. And he picked it up and balanced it on top of his snowman

and licked his fingers and said, 'Mmm, what a delicious snowball!' Then he put a hat on the top and ran home to tell his mother: 'My snowman's head tastes of cinnamon and sugar!'

But the plum pudding was still hot. It melted the snow underneath it and away it rolled again, out of the garden and down the street.

'A ball!' shouted a milkmaid to her sister, and they put down their buckets and rushed to have a game, a Christmas game of catch. The ball was slippery and heavy and when they licked their fingers they said, 'Mmm, what a delicious football!'

When the plum pudding flew past the window of the

schoolroom, everyone inside threw down their slates and chalk and ran out into the street to join in the game. Even the schoolmaster joined in. It was Christmas, after all, and no one ought to work at Christmas, Law or no Law.

One thing led to another, and soon there were people dancing and people singing carols, too. The pudding, all lovely and lardy, slipped out of a sticky pair of hands and rolled on up the street, till it came to rest outside the soldiers' barracks.

When the soldiers heard noisy crowds in the streets, saw no one was working, saw everyone was making holiday, they rattled their pikes and they drew their swords and they rolled out a cannon on to the streets.

'Fee! Fie! You wicked, lawless people!' bellowed the Sergeant. 'Stop this Christmassing or I fire!'

But the crowds only shouted back, 'Happy Christmas! Merry Christmas to you all!' and the soldiers' pikes drooped unhappily.

The Sergeant picked up a cannon ball and put it into the cannon. 'I'm warning you!' he shouted.

'Happy Christmas! Merry Christmas!' shouted back the crowd, as if they were throwing cheeky snowballs.

'I'll count to three, then I'll fire!' bellowed the Sergeant, and his soldiers put their fingers in their ears. 'One!'

'*Two!*' called the crowd. 'You wouldn't dare!'

'Oh but I would . . . *Three!*'

BANG went the cannon.

The street fell silent and filled up with smoke.

Then the smoke cleared.

The crowd stood where it had before . . . picking pieces of cannon ball out of their hair and off their faces and clothes.

'Mmm, what a delicious cannon ball!' they said.

'I do declare I can taste prunes . . .'

'. . . and cinnamon . . .'

'. . . and lard . . .'

'. . . and sugar . . .'

'. . . and orange peel . . .'

'Fee! Fie! Drat!' said the Sergeant and kicked another cannon ball.

But this time it was made of iron and not of prunes at all.

Then the crowd began to laugh, and the soldiers began to laugh, and the cats on the roofs and the rats in the drain joined in, and the birds in their cages, hung in the windows, laughed till they fell off their perches.

Someone wheeled out a barrow of oranges, and Mr Tinker pushed up his window and passed out cups of hot punch to women and men, soldiers and children alike.

What could the Sergeant do but hop about with rage and shout, 'You're under arrest! Everyone is under arrest! Everyone everywhere is under arrest!' And the town-crier, passing the end of the street, rang his handbell and called out gloomily, 'No Christ-mass! No Christ-mass! No Christ-mass, by order of the Law!'

Nobody took any notice: they were all much too busy . . . Christmassing.

27

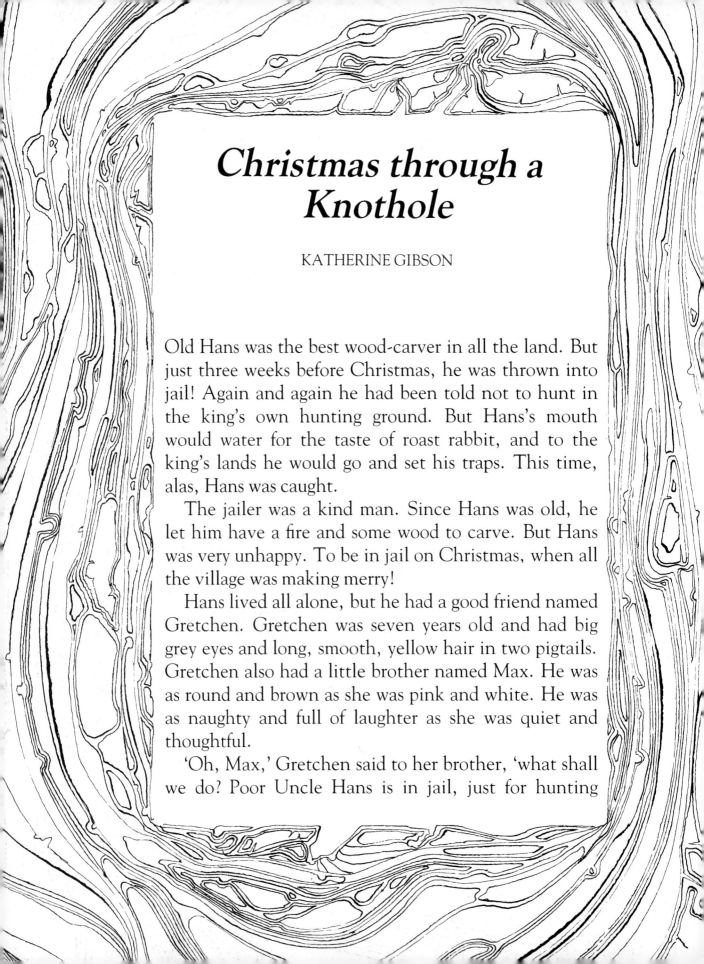

# *Christmas through a Knothole*

KATHERINE GIBSON

Old Hans was the best wood-carver in all the land. But just three weeks before Christmas, he was thrown into jail! Again and again he had been told not to hunt in the king's own hunting ground. But Hans's mouth would water for the taste of roast rabbit, and to the king's lands he would go and set his traps. This time, alas, Hans was caught.

The jailer was a kind man. Since Hans was old, he let him have a fire and some wood to carve. But Hans was very unhappy. To be in jail on Christmas, when all the village was making merry!

Hans lived all alone, but he had a good friend named Gretchen. Gretchen was seven years old and had big grey eyes and long, smooth, yellow hair in two pigtails. Gretchen also had a little brother named Max. He was as round and brown as she was pink and white. He was as naughty and full of laughter as she was quiet and thoughtful.

'Oh, Max,' Gretchen said to her brother, 'what shall we do? Poor Uncle Hans is in jail, just for hunting rabbits. He always has his Christmas dinner with us. Now he won't have any—not a bite.'

'And worse than that,' said Max, 'we won't get any toys!' For every year, of course, Old Hans carved the most wonderful toys for them.

Max looked cross. Gretchen looked sad. They walked past the jail. Like all the other houses in the village, it was made of wood. The walls were very thick, and the only window was far, far above their heads.

Suddenly Max said, 'Look, there is a hole.'

It was a large knothole in the wood. Max stood on his tiptoes and put his eye to the hole. 'I can see him. I can see Old Hans. He is carving, just the way he always does!'

'Oh, Max, let me see!' cried Gretchen. She bent down, and sure enough she could see Old Hans—or part of him.

Max took out his pocket knife (every boy in the village carried a knife) and scratched at the hole until he made it bigger. Then he put his lips to the hole and called, 'Hans, Uncle Hans, come here! Come to the knothole!'

Old Hans was surprised. He got up and followed the sound of the excited small voice. The children told him all the village news. In turn, he told them how long the days were in jail.

'It will be a sad Christmas for you, Uncle Hans,' said Gretchen. 'We will miss you at home.'

'For us it will be even worse.' Max was almost crying. 'We won't have any toys—not one!'

'You come back here tomorrow,' Uncle Hans said.

The children could hardly wait for the next day. In the morning, they hurried back to the knothole. 'Here we are, here we are, Uncle Hans,' they shouted.

The knothole was bigger now. Out of it, Uncle Hans pushed a tiny wooden figure. It was a little boy carrying a flower in his hand.

'Oh,' cried Max, 'it is just like me!'

'Only you never carry flowers,' said Gretchen. 'You just carry big sticks.'

The next day, a fat duck came through the knothole. Then a market woman. 'Why,' said Gretchen, 'that is old Martha!'

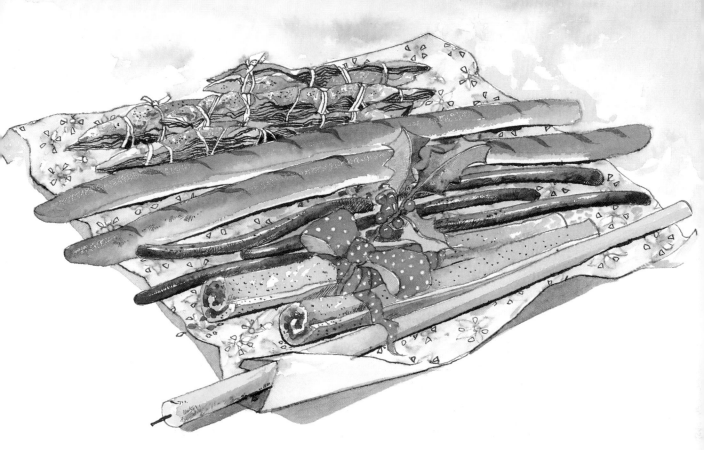

Day after day, the tiny carved figures came through the knothole. At last the children had a whole village. And not one toy was more than three inches high.

'Uncle Hans has done so much for us,' said Gretchen. 'I wonder, can we make him a knothole Christmas dinner?'

They talked with their mother. And this is what they did. They wrapped some fine pieces of roast goose into long thin bundles, four of them. They took some long, thin sausages that Hans liked ever so much. Gretchen baked some rolls. They were a very funny shape, not very different from the sausages, long and thin. Even the Christmas cakes were rolled up tight, with sugar and nuts inside.

31

'And a tall, thin candle—a Christmas candle. I will make it myself,' said Max. And he did.

Christmas Eve came. There was snow on the pointed roofs of the houses, and on the pointed tops of the fir trees. Just as the lights were lit, Max and Gretchen went to the jail.

They called Old Hans. He came and gave them the prettiest toy of all. It was a funny, fat, little fellow with a star on his head—a Christmas angel. Then Max pushed, and Gretchen pushed, and soon Hans's Christmas dinner was inside the jail. Last of all, Max pushed through the candle.

'Made it myself!' he said proudly, jumping up and down.

The children said they had never had such toys, never. And they loved them because they were so tiny. And Hans said the best dinner he ever had was the Christmas dinner through a knothole.

# Washing Their Socks

DENNIS HAMLEY

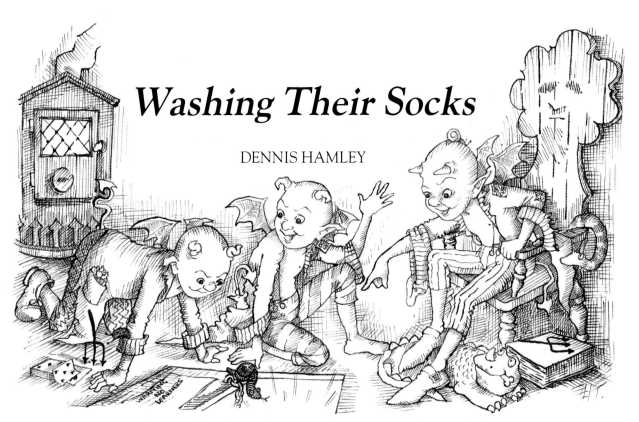

The little devils sat in the little devils' room, out of the way of the big devils. They were looking through a hole in the floor at Earth far below.

'Christmas is coming,' said Bagnose.

'The usual mess-up,' said Wartscratcher.

'It's all right if they just eat too much, get drunk and feel ill. It's when they take it seriously that trouble starts,' said Gristlethump.

'We need someone who can foul things up just as they're doing something right for a change,' said Bagnose.

'Who do you suggest?' said Wartscratcher.

They looked through the hole in the floor and concentrated hard. Then—'JANEY JAMESON!' they all shouted together.

33

'Janey, I want you to sing a solo in the carol concert,' said Miss Dibbs.

Janey's face lit up. The class chattered, nudged each other and laughed. Miss Dibbs sighed. Janey had a lovely voice and learned fast. But—she was Janey. Who knew what to expect next?

'What's it going to be, miss?' said Janey.

'Something Christmassy and nice.'

'Can't I do a Christmas rap with Leroy?'

'I wouldn't do rap with you, girl,' said Leroy in disgust.

'No, Janey. I'll decide later.'

Miss Dibbs hadn't wanted to do a carol concert. The Headteacher had insisted.

'The parents are tired of your way-out plays every year,' she said. 'We want some good old-fashioned carols and readings from the Christmas story.'

Miss Dibbs sighed. She seemed to be sighing a lot that year. If the Headteacher wanted tradition, that's what she was going to get.

34

'Oh, lovely, Janey,' said Mum. 'I *am* proud of you. We'll be in the front row, won't we, Harry?'

'I sang carol solos when I was a boy,' said Dad.

'Go on, Harry,' said Mum. 'They'd never let you.'

'Oh, yes, I did,' said Dad. Then, at the top of his voice:

'Good King Wenceslas looked out
On the Feast of Stephen;
A snowball hit him on the snout
And made it all uneven.
Brightly shone his conk that night
Though the pain was cruel,
Till the doctor came in sight
Riding on a mu-oo-el.'

Janey was impressed.

'Do you know any more like that?' she said.

Miss Dibbs was planning the concert. The reception children would start it off. Then the middle infants would sing 'Away in a Manger'. The lower juniors would do something with tambourines and xylophones because everyone would expect it. She must get Leroy and his group to do a Gospel song. The Headteacher would want to play the piano. She would ask the secondary school choir to sing something. Co-operation between schools was all the rage nowadays. It would do the children good to see what they were in for later. Then there were all the readings to arrange. That left Janey's solo. Perhaps that lovely Spanish carol she heard once.

35

'Janey Jameson singing a solo?' cried the Headteacher. 'Miss Dibbs, is this wise?'

'She has a lovely voice.'

'Give her something she can do no harm in.'

'I do need something well-known for everybody to join in. Janey could sing the first verse on her own and the audience could sing the rest. "Once in Royal David's City"?'

'Too long,' said the Headteacher.

'Well, something simple.'

'I'll consent to "While Shepherds Watched". That should be safe enough. That girl's got the devil in her.'

'Is that all?'

'It's very important, Janey. You start all the mums and dads off on their singing.'

'It's *ordinary*. Anyone can sing *that*. I want something so people will say, "That Janey Jameson! She should be on TV".'

'Everyone will say you're lovely, Janey. They'll never forget you.'

'I'll make sure they won't.'

'A *wise choice*,' said Bagnose.

'She's the girl,' said Wartscratcher.

'Doing well,' said Gristlethump.

The Christmas tree and the crib were done. The glittery decorations were put up.

'Wonderful,' said the Headteacher to Miss Dibbs. 'Every year it's the same, yet it always feels like the very first time.'

Miss Dibbs wasn't listening. She had to get the order right for the programme to be duplicated. The secondary school choir could be at the very end, to get them on and off the stage easily. So the reception children would be first. What about Leroy? And what about the Headteacher and Janey? Well, the community singing would have to be last but one, before the big choir.

Miss Dibbs sighed yet again. Things, she thought, are so *difficult*.

The last item on the programme said *Secondary School Choir—Carol*. Whenever Miss Dibbs rang up to find out what it was, the Head of Music couldn't be found. But after the programmes were printed, the phone rang.

'We're doing "The Coventry Carol". We've just learnt it. We're rather proud of ourselves.'

Miss Dibbs put the phone down and nearly wept. What a way to send people home that was. She'd wanted them to be *happy*.

'They'll never forget *me*,' said Leroy.

'They'll all forget me,' said Janey. 'What shall I do?'

'*You'll think of something, Janey,*' *said Bagnose.*

'*I'm putting a thought in her head now,*' *said Wart-scratcher.*

'*Make it a good one,*' *said Gristlethump.*

'*Quick,*' *said Bagnose.* '*Close up the floor. I hear big devils coming. You know they don't like us interfering.*'

*When Beelzebub looked round the door, all the little devils seemed very busy. Bagnose was growing deadly nightshade on blotting paper. Wartscratcher was preparing his slug table. Gristlethump was reading his instruction manual—*Humans: How to Haunt, Harry and Hassle Them Book I.

*Beelzebub glared at them suspiciously and all seven of his eyes turned red. Nobody fooled him.*

The hall was packed for the carol concert. Miss Dibbs
made sure all her performers were in their right places
and that the secondary school choir was waiting quietly
in a separate room. She was terrified. Something would
go wrong. Janey was being too nice and quiet.

The reception children sang, 'We Wish you a Merry
Christmas'. Everyone said, 'Aaaah!' The middle infants
sang 'Away in a Manger' and the lower juniors banged
their tambourines and hit their xylophones and every-

39

one clapped. Leroy and his group sang a Gospel song and everyone cheered and stamped. The Headteacher played three pieces on the piano. Everyone clapped; not too loudly.

Now it was time for everyone to join in. Things were going too well, thought Miss Dibbs as she sat at the piano. Janey stood ready, looking pretty and innocent.

You'll never forget *this*, thought Janey.

Her parents sat at the front, smiling. Janey caught Dad's eye and smiled back. Well, he told me, she thought. So it's his fault.

Her clear, true voice filled the hall.

'While shepherds washed their socks by night
All watching ITV,
The Angel of the Lord came down
And switched to BBC.'

*Beelzebub opened the hole in the floor and looked through it. Bagnose, Wartscratcher and Gristlethump cowered and snivelled in a corner.*

*'What have you done?' Beelzebub roared. 'Do you understand nothing?'*

For half a second after Janey had finished, there was silence. Miss Dibbs sat, her hands poised above the keys.

Then all the kids on stage burst into cheering and stamping. The Headteacher turned purple. Half the audience was laughing. The other half looked scandalized.

'How could she do this to us?' moaned Mum. 'What would Jesus think?'

'He's probably laughing his head off,' said Dad. 'He liked a good giggle.'

The Headteacher stood up and walked threateningly towards Janey. Miss Dibbs nearly wept again. Then she thought—courage! This needs a cool head and a firm hand. I'd better get all my kids off stage and the big ones on quickly.

The secondary school choir was ready. The audience was still buzzing; the Headteacher still a deep purple. The conductor decided to get on with it without waiting for quiet.

'Now see what you've done,' said Beelzebub. 'Half are laughing; half are shocked. Now they'll all listen. And then they'll think. *That's* the last thing we want.'

The sad, beautiful melody quietened everybody. Yes, they listened.

Lully, lulla, thou little tiny child
By by, lully lullay.

O sisters too
How may we do
 For to preserve this day
This poor youngling
For whom we do sing
 By by, lully, lullay?

Herod the king
In his raging,
 Charged he hath this day
His men of might
In his own sight
 All young children to slay.

Then woe is me,
Poor child, for thee,
 And ever mourn and may
For thy parting
Neither say nor sing
 By by, lully, lullay.

42

The people went home very quietly, thinking that
perhaps Christmas wasn't just fun and food and
presents. Once, something terrible had happened at
Christmas, yet Christmas was supposed to mean it
wouldn't happen ever again. But it did, year after year.
And, deep down, they wondered if it was time to do
something about it.

'Thank God it's over,' said Miss Dibbs.

'The best concert ever,' said Leroy. 'They'll never forget *me*.'

'And they won't forget *me*,' said Janey.

'I am prepared to forget,' said the Headteacher.

*As for Bagnose, Wartscratcher and Gristlethump, they said nothing. Ever again.*

# Jon and the Nine Yule Nisse

HELEN EAST

Wintertime in Iceland. Day and night it was dark and cold. The scattered farms and homesteads at the foot of the great volcano, Hekla, were half buried in snow. But Christmas was coming, so people smiled as they busied themselves smoking meat, curing fish and stirring puddings and preparing for their feasts on Christmas Eve.

Only in one house there were no smiles or Yuletide cheer. A mingy old man and his stingy old wife sat planning their feast in secret, plotting to keep it to themselves. In the cowshed, cold and hungry, their young foster-son Jon shivered, all on his own in the dark.

High up in the heart of smoking Hekla, warm beneath the snow and ice, nine horny, hairy trolls lay snoring in a heap. The Yule Nisse brothers, each as bad as the others, stirred in their sleep as Christmas approached:

48

Door Sniffer, Sausage Swiper,
Pot Scraper, Meat Snatcher,
Skyr Gobbler, Spoon Licker,
Hem Blower, Window Peeper,
And Candle Grabber.

Door Sniffer was the first to wake. 'Only nine days to Christmas,' he grinned, 'and today is my day.' And with a snort and a snuffle he was out and away, following his nose through the ice and the snow down to the farmsteads below. It was late when he came to the mean old woman's house, but she was still awake, busy hiding her Christmas sausage out of sight of hungry visitors.

'There!' she said, as she tucked it away in the blanket box. 'Safe as houses.'

'Quite so!' said a gruff and snuffly voice.

The old woman spun round, listening carefully. Something was sniffling and spying under the door, but when she flung it open whatever it was had gone.

Or had it?

For now she thought she heard it behind her, sniggering under the pantry door.

Try as she might, she couldn't catch it.

'You're imagining things!' snapped her husband grumpily when she woke him up to help.

But out in the cowshed Jon heard the snufflings like a warm breath whispering through his dreams, keeping him company in the dark.

Next morning the old woman got up early to check that all was well. But someone had woken even earlier. Sausage Swiper, the second Yule Nisse, had slipped down the slopes to join his brother. And the first thing he swiped was the sausage in the blanket box. The old woman howled and stamped with rage when she found it had been stolen away.

'So someone *was* watching last night!' she cried. 'It must have been that good-for-nothing boy, Jon. There's no one else around for miles.'

So poor Jon got the blame as usual and was sent to bed that night without any supper. As he lay in the hay, too hungry to sleep, he thought about the missing sausage. If only he *had* eaten it! Mmmm . . . He imagined it, all hot and spicy. He could almost taste it. He could certainly smell it. It seemed so real.

It *was* real.

He sat up with a start as a Christmas sausage brushed past his nose.

'Go on! Have a bite,' something said in his ear, in the warm, whispering voice he had heard in his dreams.

'Don't worry. Just hurry,' a second voice added. 'Or there won't be any left.'

Even if it was a dream, Jon decided, it was too good to waste.

Never in his life had he tasted such a delicious sausage, or met two such peculiar creatures as the Yule Nisse. It was too dark to see, but they felt strange and furry and smelt very odd. But they were so warm and friendly, Jon soon felt one of the family.

The next day the old woman decided to make her Christmas pudding, which in Iceland is a rice pudding with raisins in if you're lucky. This time she was determined to take no chances, so Jon was sent off all day looking for lost sheep. Even the old man was out, gathering moss for the fire. The wife drew the curtains and set to work. Soon the kitchen was filled with the rich milky smell of baked pudding.

'It must be done now,' she thought, and went to lift it off the stove.

But the pot was empty, scraped clean as a bone.

'I'll skin that boy alive!' she screamed, grabbing a thick stick and forgetting that she'd already sent Jon far away.

Of course, she never thought of looking up the chimney, so she never saw Pot Scraper, the third Yule Nisse, licking his fingers and smiling blissfully.

'Done to a turn,' he sighed, and burped happily.

If the wife was upset, the old man was even worse. He was just as mean and greedy as she was, and the thought of something or someone getting his food made him bubble and boil with rage. He stared anxiously at the large leg of lamb that hung smoking over the fire. Smoked lamb is the traditional Christmas meal for Icelanders and this one looked especially rich and tasty. The old man drooled at the thought of biting into it.

'No one will steal this,' he decided. 'I'll make sure of that!'

All evening he watched it carefully, and that night he took it to bed with him, placing it under his pillow.

'That will take care of that!' he said to his wife.

But as he snored and twitched in the early hours of the morning a long hairy hand slipped stealthily under his pillow.

The lamb was indeed delicious, as Jon and the Nisse agreed when they gathered round in the cowshed for their nightly Yuletide feast.

So day by day—and night by night—life got better for Jon but worse for the stingy couple. Skyr Gobbler snatched the yoghourt-skyr from under the old woman's nose. Spoon Licker licked their spoons right out of their hands.

Hem Blower crept in through the cracks and gaps. He blew icy draughts up skirts and trouser legs and tangled the old woman's hair and the old man's beard into hundreds of knots. And all night long he banged open doors and lifted the quilts off beds.

And Window Peeper seemed to have eyes everywhere, first at one window, then another, then all the windows at once. It was no use drawing curtains or shutting shutters, the old couple could feel his eyes peering through, always watching whatever they did. By the end of his day they were jumping at shadows, their nerves torn to shreds.

But out in the cowshed, night after night, the feasting and fun grew wilder and wilder. Window Peeper told stories of the things he had seen on his travels. Hem Blower whistled like the wind. Spoon Licker could touch his eyebrows with his tongue. Jon laughed until he ached. For once in his life, he was happy.

So eight days passed and Christmas Eve came, the day of feasting and dancing in Iceland. In the morning the old woman sent Jon out, trudging through the snow and ice from farm to farm to beg and borrow more food for Christmas. The neighbours gave generously and Jon returned laden with lamb, skyr, dried fish and even a small bowl of pudding. But still the mean old couple didn't want the boy to share the feast.

'He eats too much,' muttered the old man.

'It's wasted on him,' added the old woman.

'Let's get him out of the way,' they agreed.

Pretending to be friendly, the woman called Jon inside. 'Here's your Christmas gift,' she said. 'A candle to burn at church.'

It was only a half-burnt stump of candle, but Jon was delighted. Now he could go to the churchyard with everyone else to decorate the graves with candles. On

Christmas Eve, so they say, trolls and elves and ghosts and all the Hidden Folk come out of the ground to enjoy themselves. So people light candles to welcome back the ghosts of long lost friends and relatives.

As soon as he had gone, the old woman shut and bolted the door and the old man pushed a heavy table against it.

'Now light the candles,' cried the old woman, 'and we can feast.'

She began unpacking the food while the old man lit the candles.

The candles lit, the table laid, they sat down with a grin. But before they could take their first bite, the candles flickered and died. Grumbling, the old man reached to relight them—then stopped, fumbling in mid air. The candlesticks were there, but they were empty. Candle Grabber, the last of the Nine, had come down from the mountain to join his brothers.

'Well, we'll eat in the dark,' said the greedy old man.

'Build up the fire bright,' said the old woman.

'Oh no you won't,' said a voice.

'Oh no you don't,' said another.

'Something's pinching me,' squealed the old woman.

'Something's scratching me,' moaned the old man.

'Something's poking me,' sobbed the old woman.

'Something's kicking me!'

'Hitting me!'

'ow!'

'Let's get out of here!'

They ran to the door, but the table was blocking it. As they fought to get by they were attacked on all sides by nine roaring, screeching, spitting, hissing Yule Nisse.

'We'll eat you alive for our feast,' they howled.

The old man and his wife might never have got out if Jon had not come back that very moment. With one easy push he opened the door and the old couple tumbled out in a heap.

'Whatever's the matter?' asked Jon.

But the mean old man and the mingy old woman didn't even stop to explain. They just picked themselves up and ran for their lives, through the snow and bitter weather over the hills and away. And if they haven't stopped yet they must be running still for nobody ever saw them again. So Jon got the farm and everything with it (including the Yule Nisse). And what a feast they had to celebrate!

All through the long Christmas night they sang and danced and told such stories that even great Hekla herself rumbled and shook with laughter.

# Brer Rabbit's Christmas

## JOEL CHANDLER HARRIS

Once upon a bright clear winter morning Brer Fox stole into Brer Rabbit's garden and dug up a big sackful of his best carrots. Brer Rabbit didn't see him as he was visiting his friend Brer Bear at the time. When he got home he was mighty angry to see his empty carrot-patch.

'Brer Fox! That's who's been here,' cried Brer Rabbit, and his whiskers twitched furiously. 'Here are his paw marks and some hairs from his tail. All my best winter carrots gone! I'll make him give them back or my name's not Brer Rabbit.'

He went along, lippity lip, clippity clip, and as he went along his little nose wrinkled at the fragrant smell of soup coming from Brer Fox's house.

'Now see here,' he called crossly. 'I just know it's my carrots you're cooking. I want them back, so you'd better open your door.'

'Too bad,' chuckled Brer Fox. 'I'm not opening my door until winter is over. I have plenty of carrots,

58

thanks to my kind friend Brer Rabbit, and a stack of other food for Christmas as well. I'm keeping my windows shut and my door bolted, so do go away. I want to enjoy my first bowl of carrot soup in peace.'

At this, Brer Rabbit kicked the door, blim blam. He hammered on the door, bangety bang. It wasn't any use. My, he was in a rage as he turned away. Kind friend Brer Rabbit, indeed! He stomped off, muttering furiously. But soon he grew thoughtful, then he gave a hop or two followed by a little dance. By the time he reached home he was in a mighty good temper. Brer

Rabbit had a plan all worked out. He'd get his carrots back and annoy Brer Fox into the bargain!

On Christmas Eve, Brer Rabbit heaved a sack of stones on his shoulder and climbed up onto Brer Fox's roof. He clattered round the chimney, making plenty of noise.

'Who's there?' Brer Fox called. 'Go away at once. I'm cooking my supper.'

'It's Father Christmas,' replied Brer Rabbit in a gruff voice. 'I've brought a sack full of presents for Brer Fox.'

'Oh, that's different,' said Brer Fox quickly. 'You're most welcome. Come right along down the chimney.'

'I can't. I'm stuck,' Brer Rabbit said in his gruff Father Christmas voice. Brer Fox unbolted his door and went outside to take a look. Certainly he could see somebody on the roof, so he rushed back inside and called, 'Well, Father Christmas, don't trouble to come down the chimney yourself. Just drop the sack of presents and I'll surely catch it.'

'Can't. That's stuck too,' yelled Brer Rabbit and he smiled to himself. 'You'll have to climb up inside your chimney, Brer Fox, then catch hold of the piece of string around the sack and you can haul it down yourself.'

'That's easy,' Brer Fox cried, 'here I come,' and he disappeared up the chimney.

Like lightning, Brer Rabbit was off that roof and in through the open doorway. There were his carrots in a sack, and on the table was a fine cooked goose and a huge Christmas pudding. He grabbed them both, stuffed them into the sack and he ran. Chickle, chuckle, how he did run.

That old Brer Fox struggled up the chimney, higher and higher. He couldn't see any string but he felt it hanging down so he gave a big tug. The sack opened and out tumbled all the stones, clatter bang, bim, bam, right on Brer Fox's head. My, my, he certainly went down that chimney quickly. Poor Brer Fox! He'd lost his Christmas dinner and the carrots, and now he had a sore head.

That rascally Brer Rabbit laughed and laughed but he made sure he kept out of Brer Fox's way all that Christmas Day and for some time afterwards.

# *Beginning Christmas*

RACHEL HANDS

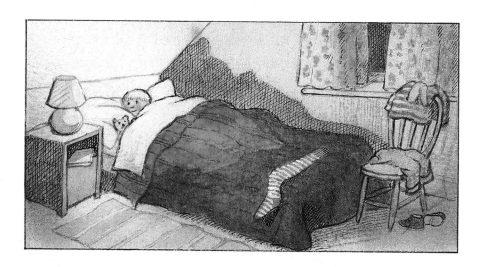

It was Christmas Eve.

Jamie had slept in the car almost all the way to Grandma's. Now it was bed-time and he was wide awake.

'Read a little,' said Mum, giving him his book.

'Try counting sheep,' said Grandpa, and Grandma said: 'Have some hot milk and a biscuit.'

'Just *pretend* to be asleep,' said Dad, 'and you soon will be.'

But Jamie grew more and more excited, and more and more awake.

His stocking hung at the end of the bed, but Father Christmas would never come while anyone was awake.

He lay with his eyes open . . .

                   . . . and with them shut.

He lay with the light on . . .

                   . . . and with it off.

He curled up tight . . .

                 . . . and he stretched out flat.

He tried *everything*, and *still* he couldn't sleep.

He counted sheep, and they turned into Christmas presents in his head. He sang himself lullabies, and they turned into Christmas carols.

He went to the bathroom, and from the landing he could see the decorations in Grandma's hall.

'I *can't* go to sleep,' he wailed. 'And Christmas will *never* come.'

'Yes it will,' said Dad, coming upstairs. He had his thick coat on again, and his scarf and gloves.

'Are you going out?' asked Jamie, surprised.

'Yes,' said Dad. 'And you can come with me. Christmas is coming, and I must go and help. You can come and watch.'

He helped Jamie put on his thickest jersey, and two pairs of socks. Downstairs, they pulled on his boots and anorak.

'I can't go out in my *pyjamas*,' said Jamie.

'No one will notice,' said Dad.

Grandma and Grandpa were already asleep when Mum saw them quietly out of the house.

It was dark, but there was a bright moon, and the ground sparkled and crunched as they walked.

'It's a bit icy,' said Dad. 'Be careful not to slip.' And he held Jamie's hand as they crept down the path.

In the road, a few cars went by, and then it was quiet.

'Where are we going?' whispered Jamie.

'To begin Christmas,' said Dad. 'I did this every year, when I lived here.'

They came to the church. Inside, it was silent and warm. No candles were lit, and only one light was on. In the darkness, Jamie could smell the holly and the ivy, and the Christmas flowers and the unlit candles. No one was there.

They went to a small door at the back. It was open,
and inside were stone steps, going up into the dark.

Then Jamie knew.

'You're going to ring the bells,' he said. 'Like at
home, on Sundays.'

'That's right,' said Dad.

'But in the middle of the *night?*' asked Jamie.

'Yes,' said Dad. 'For Christmas. Christmas begins at
night.'

'Can I ring them too?' asked Jamie.

'No,' said Dad. 'You're too little.'

Then he stopped in the doorway and spoke to Jamie. His face was very solemn. 'Listen, Jamie: you're too little, really, even to come and watch. Little children don't come into the ringing chamber, because they might get hurt. But Mum thinks, and I think, that you are big enough to be grown-up and sensible, and do just what I say. All right?'

'Yes,' said Jamie, and his face was as solemn as Dad's.

They went out of the warm church, and up the cold dark stairs. Jamie was frightened, and held tight to Dad as they climbed round and round. He was glad when they stepped out into a room where the light was on, and people were talking.

'This is the ringing chamber,' said Dad. 'You can sit on this bench.' And he pulled him into a corner beside him.

'You can watch all you like,' he said, 'but you mustn't call out, and you *must* keep still, with your feet tucked out of the way. And whatever happens, you must NOT touch the ropes.'

'Yes, Dad,' said Jamie, and pushed himself further into his corner.

Now some of the people were standing in a ring, holding the ropes.

'Look to,' said one. 'Treble's going. She's gone—'

Quickly, one after another, they pulled the ropes, pulled again, caught them, and pulled again.

Somewhere, the bells began to ring:
*Ding dong ding dong ding dong*
*Ding dong ding dong ding dong*

'Where *are* the bells?' whispered Jamie, but just then one of the men called out, and the tune seemed to change:

Ding dong ding dong ding dong—
Dong ding dong ding dong ding
Dong dong ding dong ding ding—

'Where *are* they?' asked Jamie again, and Dad said: 'Up there in the roof, where the ropes are going.'

Jamie watched for a bit, but the ropes wriggling so fast through the holes made him feel funny, and he watched the people again.

They rang on and on and on. Now and again somebody called out, but nobody seemed to take any notice. The fat red and blue stripes on the ropes began to dance before Jamie's eyes.

At last they stopped. Dad got up and spoke to a big girl, who gave him her rope and came to sit by Jamie. Other people changed places, and they began again.

'Look to. Treble's going. She's gone—'

Ding dong ding dong ding dong
Ding dong ding dong ding dong—

'Why do they have the stripy thing on the rope?' asked Jamie, and the big girl said, 'It's soft, and easy to catch. It's called the sally.'

Jamie laughed. Dad had called their cat Sally. Now he thought of her tail, and knew why.

Suddenly the noise of the bells changed, and everyone was shouting and calling out and stepping forward into the middle.

68

*Ding dong-a ding-a-dong-a-dong CRASH!*
*Ding dong-a-ding CRASH dong CRASH!*

'It's all right,' said the girl, holding tight to Jamie. 'Someone went wrong. Not your Dad. He's helping to put them right.'

Jamie listened while the noise got sorted out. 'That was *awful*,' he said. He wriggled back into his corner, and noticed something.

'I've got my pyjamas on,' he whispered.

The big girl looked down.

'I thought it was a tracksuit,' she said.

Now the bells were ringing sweetly again. Jamie began to feel tired, and his pyjamas made him feel sleepy. The big girl put her arm around him . . .

When he woke up, the ringing had stopped. People were putting their coats on again and talking.

'Happy Christmas!' they said. 'Happy Christmas, Jamie. Jim'll have to teach *you* to ring when you're bigger. Happy Christmas!'

'Happy Christmas!' said Jamie, and then to Dad: 'Has it begun now?'

'Yes,' said Dad. 'Listen!' and through the floor they heard the organ in the church playing 'Hark, the Herald Angels Sing'.

'It's just beginning,' said Dad. 'Come on.'

Down the cold stone stairs they went, round and round, and out into the warm church.

Now all the lights were on and the candles were lit, and it was full of people standing up and singing.

'Are we going to church *now?*' asked Jamie. 'In the middle of the night?'

'No,' said Dad. 'It's too late, and you're too little. We'll come back in the morning.'

They crept out past all the people.

'Anyway,' said Jamie, 'I'm in my pyjamas.'

In the porch the ringers said goodnight to each other.

'See you in the morning.' 'Don't be late.' 'Happy Christmas!'

'Happy Christmas!' they said to Dad and Jamie, and 'Happy Christmas!' said Dad and Jamie as they set off to walk home.

It was further than Jamie remembered, and Dad had to carry him the last bit.

In the hall, Mum took off his boots and socks and anorak, and carried him upstairs. Then she took off his jersey, and tucked him into bed.

'Christmas has come,' said Jamie. 'It's begun. It begins at night.'

'That's right,' said his mother, 'and in the morning it will be Christmas day.'

Jamie snuggled down in Grandma's funny fold-up bed. He remembered something. He sat up again.

'Mum,' he called. 'Christmas has begun, and I went to watch, and I went all down the road and into the church *in my pyjamas!*'

He lay down and went to sleep.

# Gifts

ADÈLE GERAS

It was late on Christmas Eve. Rachel lay in bed, wide awake, wondering why the time went by so slowly when you very much wanted it to go quickly. She had tried all the tricks she could think of for getting to sleep: counting sheep, saying her numbers backwards starting from 100, going through her favourite nursery rhymes, but nothing seemed to work. The landing light made a golden triangle on Rachel's carpet and the ornaments on her chest-of-drawers all had black shadows stretching out behind them.

'I wish,' Rachel said aloud, 'that there was someone to talk to.'

'There is,' said a voice. 'You can talk to us.'

'Who's that?' Rachel sat up in her bed and looked all round the room.

'It's me,' said a small wooden camel. 'Your camel, up on the chest-of-drawers.'

'I didn't know you could speak,' Rachel said. 'Are you quite sure I'm not dreaming?'

'All animals, even ones made of wood and clay and metal, can speak on Christmas Eve,' said the camel. 'It's the magic in the air. And, of course, the lion lies down with the lamb, and the wolf with the young kid. There are no hunters and hunted on Christmas Eve. All the animals are friends, just for this one night.'

'Even cats and mice?'

'Even them.'

'And foxes and chickens?' Rachel asked.

'Even them,' the camel said.

'How wonderful,' said Rachel. 'What shall we talk about?'

'I was going to tell all my friends about my great adventure,' said the camel.

'Yes, please do,' said a tiny copper elephant. 'We've all been wondering where you disappeared to. You were gone for a whole week.'

'Yes,' said a rooster painted all over with red flowers, 'one day you were up here with all of us, and the next, you were nowhere to be seen.'

'Rachel picked you up,' said a porcelain frog, 'and ran out of the room. We've been longing to ask you all about it.'

'I know where he went,' said Rachel. 'I'll tell you . . .'

'Ssh!' said a mouse made from a cluster of seashells. 'Let Camel tell us himself.'

'I went to Rachel's school,' said Camel. 'All the children in her class were making a Nativity scene to decorate the classroom. Everyone had brought something. One boy brought cotton wool to make clouds out of.'

'That was Vivek,' said Rachel. 'His dad has a clothes out of. . .'

'Another little girl had pretty material to make clothes out of. . . .'

'That was Sharon. Her mother does a lot of sewing,' Rachel told the listening animals. 'And Patsy brought straw, because she's got a rabbit.'

'Marion and Jack brought a lot of plastic farm animals,' said Camel. 'And Rachel brought me. At first, some of the children thought I shouldn't be in the Nativity scene.'

'But then,' Rachel interrupted him, 'Mrs Ellison explained to the class that there were lots of camels in Bethlehem where Jesus was born, and I told everyone that you'd been sent to me by my grandmother who lives in Jerusalem, as a gift. Jerusalem is very near Bethlehem, so you became very important.'

Camel coughed modestly. 'I had a little notice pinned to the table beside my feet. It said: "This camel comes from the Holy Land. It is carved from the wood of the olive tree. Jesus would have seen many olive trees and many camels during His lifetime." It was a beautiful Nativity scene. Everybody said so.'

'Yes, they did,' Rachel agreed. 'And at the end of term, some of the things we used in the scene were given out as presents. I got one of the extra sheep, made out of a cotton reel with cotton wool stuck over it. Rukshana gave me the star, which was pinned to the roof of the stable. Look!'

Rachel took the star, which was really a brooch belonging to Rukshana's mother, from its place of honour on her bedside table and held it up for all the animals to see. It glittered in the light and threw small rainbows into the corner of the room.

'How kind of Rukshana!' said the copper elephant. 'What a lovely gift! What are you going to give her?'

Rachel hung her head. 'I don't know what to give her. I don't even know if her family has gifts at Christmas, and anyway, all the shops are closed now.'

'Gifts given at Christmas time are lovely,' said the flowered rooster. 'It doesn't matter at all whether you always have presents at Christmas or not. I was a Christmas gift myself.'

'So was I,' said the copper elephant. 'I'd only been one of a herd of elephants on the shelf in the Oxfam shop until your father chose me for you. Oh, I was

74

excited! How wonderful to be wrapped in paper with pictures on it, and unwrapped by a real child! Heavenly!'

'But I can't give one of you to Rukshana as a present. I'd miss you,' Rachel said.

'What about the toy snowstorm?' asked the porcelain frog. 'It's a very pretty ornament. I'm sure anyone would want to have it. You think it's beautiful, don't you?'

Rachel loved the snowstorm. It stood right at the back of the chest-of-drawers, up near the wall and half-hidden by a china pig. Rukshana, whenever she came to play, used to look and look at the way the snowflakes whirled around the little castle, and drifted over the tiny princess who stood in front of it in a long blue and silver dress. Rachel knew she would miss it, but she thought of how happy Rukshana would be when she saw it, and that made her feel better.

'You're brilliant, Frog!' she cried. 'I'll wrap it up tomorrow and take it to Rukshana's house. I'll just lie down for a moment, now. . .'

Rachel closed her eyes, and heard, before she fell into a deep sleep, the small voices of her ornaments rising and falling and fading away.

The next afternoon, Rachel took the snowstorm to Rukshana's house. It was wrapped in shiny red paper.

'I've brought you a Christmas present,' she said to Rukshana.

'Thank you,' said Rukshana, 'but I don't really have Christmas presents. We don't really have a proper Christmas.'

'But you gave me your mother's brooch. That was a Christmas gift, wasn't it?'

'No,' said Rukshana. 'That was just a gift given at Christmas time.'

'So is this,' said Rachel. 'I want you to have it.'

'Thank you, then,' said Rukshana. 'What is it?'

'Open it and see.'

Rukshana opened the parcel and shook the snow-storm until the flakes filled the air around the castle, and the little princess had almost vanished.

'It's your beautiful ornament!' said Rukshana. 'You know I love it. Thank you so much. And look,' she pointed over Rachel's head at the iron grey sky. 'It's just beginning to snow here. Isn't that lovely? Maybe it's a magic gift. If we stay on the doorstep, we'll look just like the princess.'

'But we'll get cold,' said Rachel. 'I'd rather be a princess indoors.'

'Come and play inside, then,' said Rukshana.

All afternoon, as the snowflakes fell and floated outside, the two girls pretended that they were wearing blue and silver dresses and living in the little castle in Rukshana's toy snowstorm.

# Anderson the Carpenter and Father Christmas

ALF PRØYSEN

There was once a carpenter called Anderson. He was a good father and he had a lot of children.

One Christmas Eve, while his wife and children were decorating the Christmas tree, Anderson crept out to his woodshed. He had a surprise for them all: he was going to dress up as Father Christmas, load a sack of presents on to his sledge and go and knock on the front door. But as he pulled the loaded sledge out of the woodshed, he slipped and fell right across the sack of presents. This set the sledge moving, because the ground sloped from the shed down to the road, and Anderson had no time even to shout, 'Way there!' before he crashed into another sledge, coming down the road.

'I'm very sorry,' said Anderson.

'Don't mention it; I couldn't stop myself,' said the other man. Like Anderson, he was dressed in Father Christmas clothes and had a sack on his sledge.

'We seem to have had the same idea,' said Anderson.

78

'I see you're all dressed up like me.' He laughed and shook the other man's hand. 'My name's Anderson.'

'Glad to meet you,' said the other. 'I'm Father Christmas.'

'Ha, ha!' laughed Anderson. 'You will have your little joke, and quite right too on a Christmas Eve.'

'That's what I thought,' said the other man, 'and if you agree we can change places tonight, and that will be a better joke still; I'll take the presents along to *your* children, if you'll go and visit *mine*. But you must take off that costume.'

Anderson looked a bit puzzled. 'What am I to dress up in, then?'

'You don't need to dress up at all,' said the other. 'My children see Father Christmas all the year round, but they've never seen a real carpenter. I told them last Christmas that if they were good this year I'd try and get the carpenter to come and see them while I went round with presents for the other children.'

So he really *is* Father Christmas, thought Anderson to himself. Out loud he said: 'All right, if you really want me to, I will. The only thing is, I haven't any presents for your children.'

'Presents?' said Father Christmas. 'Aren't you a carpenter?'

'Yes, of course.'

'Well, then, all you have to do is to take along a few pieces of wood and some nails. You have a knife, I suppose?' Anderson said he had and went to look for the things in his workshop.

'Just follow my footsteps in the snow; they'll lead you to my house in the forest,' said Father Christmas. 'Then I'll take your sack and sledge and go and knock on your door.'

'Righto!' said the carpenter.

Then Father Christmas went off to knock at Anderson's door, and the carpenter trudged through the snow following Father Christmas's footsteps. They led him into the forest, past two pine trees, a large boulder and a tree stump. There, peeping out from behind the stump, were three little faces with red caps on.

'He's here! He's here!' shouted the Christmas children as they scampered in front of him to a fallen tree, lying with its roots in the air. When Anderson followed them round to the other side of the roots he found Mother Christmas standing there waiting for him.

'Here he is, Mum! Here's the carpenter Dad promised us! Look at him! Isn't he tall!' The children were all shouting at once.

'Now, now, children,' said Mother Christmas, 'anybody would think you'd never seen a human being before.'

'We've never seen a proper *carpenter* before!' shouted the children. 'Come on in, Mr Carpenter!'

Pulling a branch aside, Mother Christmas led the way into the house. Anderson had to bend his long back double and crawl on his hands and knees. But once in, he found he could straighten up. The room had a mud floor, but it was very cosy, with tree stumps for chairs, and beds made of moss with covers of plaited grass. In the smallest bed lay the Christmas baby and in the far corner sat a very old Grandfather Christmas, his red cap nodding up and down.

'Has anyone come to see me?' croaked old Grandfather Christmas.

Mother Christmas shouted in his ear. 'It's Anderson, the carpenter!' She explained that Grandfather was so old he never went out any more. 'He'd be pleased if you came over and shook hands with him.'

So Anderson took the old man's hand, which was as hard as a piece of bark.

'Come and sit here, Mr Carpenter!' called the children.

The eldest one spoke first. 'D'you know what I want you to make for me? A toboggan. Can you do that—a little one, I mean?'

'I'll try,' said Anderson, and it didn't take long before he had a smart toboggan just ready to fly over the snow.

'Now it's my turn,' said the little girl who had pigtails sticking straight out from her head. 'I want a doll's bed.'

'Have you any dolls?' asked Anderson.

'No, but I borrow the fieldmice sometimes, and I can play with the baby squirrels as much as I like. They *love* being dolls. Please make me a doll's bed.'

So the carpenter made her a doll's bed. Then he asked the smaller boy what he would like. But he was very shy and could only whisper, 'Don't know.'

' 'Course he knows!' said his sister. 'He said it just before you came. Go on, tell the carpenter.'

'A top,' whispered the little boy.

'That's easy,' said the carpenter, and in no time at all he had made a top.

82

'And now you must make something for Mum!' said the children. Mother Christmas had been watching, but all the time she held something behind her back.

'Shush, children, don't keep bothering the carpenter,' she said.

'That's all right,' said Anderson. 'What would you like me to make?'

Mother Christmas brought out the thing she was holding; it was a wooden ladle, very worn, with a crack in it.

83

'Could you mend this for me, d'you think?' she asked.

'Hm, hm!' said Anderson, scratching his ear with his carpenter's pencil. 'I think I'd better make you a new one.' And he quickly cut a new ladle for Mother Christmas. Then he found a long twisted root with a crook at one end and started stripping it with his knife. But, although the children asked him and asked him, he wouldn't tell them what it was going to be. When it was finished he held it up; it was a very distinguished-looking walking stick.

'Here you are, Grandpa!' he shouted to the old man, and handed him the stick. Then he gathered up all the chips and made a wonderful little bird with wings outspread to hang over the baby's cot.

'How pretty!' exclaimed Mother Christmas and all the children. 'Thank the carpenter nicely now. We'll certainly never forget this Christmas Eve, will we?'

'Thank you, Mr Carpenter. Thank you very much!' shouted the children.

There was a sound of feet stamping the snow off outside the door, and Anderson knew it was time for him to go. He said goodbye all round and wished them a Happy Christmas. Then he crawled through the narrow opening under the fallen tree. Father Christmas was waiting for him. He had the sledge and the empty sack with him.

'Thank you for your help, Anderson,' he said. 'What did the youngsters say when they saw you?'

'Oh, they seemed very pleased. Now they're just waiting for you to come home and see their new toys. How did you get on at my house? Was little Peter frightened of you?'

'Not a bit,' said Father Christmas. 'He thought I was you. "Sit on Dadda's knee," he kept saying.'

'Well, I must get back to them,' said Anderson, and said goodbye to Father Christmas.

When he got home, the first thing he said to the children was, 'Can I see the presents you got from Father Christmas?'

But the children laughed. 'Silly! You've seen them already—when you were Father Christmas; you unpacked them all for us!'

'What would you say if I told you I had been with Father Christmas's family all this time?'

But the children laughed again. 'Where do they live, then?' they said.

'Just along there and over there,' said Anderson, pointing.

But it was snowing harder and harder, and very soon all of his own tracks and Father Christmas's had gone.

# The Cat on the Dovrefell

**Traditional, retold by**

ROBERT SCOTT

Once upon a time there was a man in Finnmark who came upon a white bear cub that had got lost in the snow. He took it home with him, fed it and cared for it until it was fully grown. But the larger it grew, the more frightened his neighbours became and the more difficult it was to find enough food for it. So he decided to take it as a present to the King of Denmark.

His journey took him across the Dovrefell and it was there, on Christmas Eve, that he came to the cottage of a man called Halvor. He asked Halvor if he and his bear could stay there for the night.

'No,' said Halvor, 'I'm afraid I can't ask you to stay. We're just getting ready to leave.'

'She's all right,' said the man, thinking Halvor was afraid of the bear. 'She won't cause any trouble.'

'It's not your bear,' said Halvor. 'At any other time you would be welcome, but we can't have any guests at Christmas. As you see, we can't even stay here ourselves.'

'*Can't?*' asked the man.

'You must have travelled a long way if you haven't heard of the Dovrefell,' said Halvor. 'Every Christmas Eve the trolls come down from the fells to feast themselves while we keep Christmas out in the snow. You see, we don't have a roof over our own heads, so we can't put anyone up at this time of the year.'

'If that is all,' said the man, 'we can look after your house while you're away. My bear can sleep by the stove and I'll use one of the side rooms.'

At first Halvor and his wife would not hear of it.

They knew from long experience what it was like to be visited by the trolls. But the man persisted so finally they agreed, saying they would return promptly the next day to see how he and his bear had got on.

Before they left, though, they got the feast ready. Bowls of rice porridge, dishes of dried fish, plates of smoked lamb, heaps of savoury sausages prepared specially for the Christmas feast, pork and beef, pies and cakes, ale and wine were loaded on to the table. The couple didn't expect to taste any of it, but they knew that if they didn't provide a great feast for the trolls they would return to find broken furniture and smashed pots and dishes. With last minute advice to keep quiet and stay out of sight, they gathered their bundles and moved out. The bear was already snoozing behind the stove, so the man made himself scarce in the next room.

No sooner had he done so than the trolls descended.

There were short, fat trolls and long, thin ones; trolls with big, flat feet and trolls with big, flat ears; trolls with long, twisty tails and trolls with no tails at all.

There were trolls with green eyes and trolls with green teeth; trolls with hairy hands and trolls with hairy feet; trolls with long, twisty horns and trolls with no horns at all.

There were trolls with long arms and trolls with long noses; trolls with big bellies and trolls with big bottoms; trolls with long, twisty beards and trolls with no beards at all.

And they were all hungry.

They slurped the porridge and chomped the fish.

They slobbered over the sausages and wolfed the lamb.

They gnawed the pork and bolted the beef.

They crammed pies and cakes into their big, wide mouths.

They washed it all down with strong, brown ale and dark, red wine.

And burped.

One of the baby trolls crawled from under the table and saw the bear sleeping behind the stove. He took a sausage, stuck it on a fork, and grilled it until it was sizzling hot.

'Here, puss, have a sausage!' he screeched, and poked it in the bear's nose.

The big, white bear hauled herself upright with a ferocious roar and soon all the trolls, tall and short, thin and fat, were fleeing back to their caves on the fell.

The next year Halvor was out on the afternoon of Christmas Eve cutting wood before the holidays started. After the story the man with the bear had told him, he wasn't sure whether he and his wife should prepare for the trolls or not.

'Halvor! Halvor!' A voice from the woods interrupted his chopping.

'Yes,' said Halvor. 'I'm here.'

'Halvor, have you still got that big, white cat of yours?'

Cat? Halvor remembered.

'Oh, yes I have,' he said. 'She's lying at home in her favourite place behind the stove. And what's more, she's now got seven kittens and do you know, each kitten is far bigger and far fiercer than its mother!'

'Then we shan't be coming to see you again!' shouted the troll. And they kept their word. Since that time the trolls have never come down to enjoy Halvor's Christmas feast on the Dovrefell.

# Father Christmas's Clothes

PAUL BIEGEL

Joanna's cheeks were bright red with excitement.

'Listen!' she called, 'listen to this!' She rushed across the playground. 'He's coming to stay with us. In our house!'

'Huh?' asked Sylvia. 'Stay? Who?'

'Oh,' cried Joanna, 'Father Christmas, of course.'

'Father Christmas?'

Now all the children were crowding round her. 'Did you hear that? Father Christmas is coming to stay with Joanna.'

'Ha ha! He can't. Father Christmas never stays with anyone.' That was Billy.

'He must sleep somewhere, mustn't he?' That was Maria.

'But not in people's houses!'

'No. Where, then?'

'Father Christmas doesn't sleep. He rides over the roofs at night.'

'Yes, well then, he must sleep in the daytime.'

'But not at Joanna's.'

'Yes!' cried Joanna. 'At our house. He's coming to stay with us. I saw it myself.'

'Saw what? Father Christmas?'

'No,' said Joanna, 'his clothes.' And she went on: 'The bell rang and there was a man at the door. He had a big box. And Mummy said: 'Put it in the spare room.' But she wouldn't tell me what was inside. So I went to have a look, when she wasn't watching. The box wasn't shut and Father Christmas's clothes were inside it. I saw them.'

The children stared, open-mouthed. But Billy said: 'I don't believe it.'

94

'Well,' said Joanna, 'you ask my Mum, then.'

And they did. When school came out and Joanna's mother was standing at the gate waiting to pick up Joanna, all the children ran up to her.

'Mrs Green, Mrs Green, is it true, what Joanna says? That Father Christmas is coming to stay with you?'

Joanna's mother gave them an odd look. 'How did you get that idea?' she asked.

'Ha ha! Joanna said that Father Christmas's box of clothes was brought to your house.'

'Oh,' said Joanna's mother. Her cheeks turned a little red, as well. 'Yes, that is true. I didn't know you had seen that, Joanna.'

Oh dear! Joanna's face was fiery red.

'Oh well,' said her mother. 'What you said about the box is true, but as to Father Christmas coming to stay with us . . . I don't know for sure.'

'Oh?' cried Maria, 'how funny. Then why would he have his clothes brought to your house?'

'Uhum,' said Joanna's mother. She scratched her neck thoughtfully. 'I think he must be coming, just for a day or two.'

Then she took Joanna's hand and began to walk her quickly home.

The other children could see even from a distance that Joanna was getting into trouble—because she had given the secret away, of course.

That night Joanna simply could not sleep. It's Christmas Eve the day after tomorrow, she thought. Father Christmas must have been travelling for a long time already and he will soon be here. But her mother had said that he would be much too busy to see Joanna.

'Father Christmas will only come home to sleep very late at night and he will have to be on his way again very early in the morning,' her mother said.

I shall have to be awake earlier still, thought Joanna. And I shall creep very quietly to the spare room. In her mind she could see Father Christmas lying in bed with his beard over the sheet. In *her* house. Would he snore?

But it was already late when Joanna woke up and when she looked, the spare room bed was quite smooth. The covers were all straight. Could Father Christmas have made the bed up himself before he left?

'That must be it,' said Sylvia, when Joanna told her about it. But Billy and the others did not believe it.

'He wasn't in your house at all,' they said. 'And he won't be coming, either.'

Joanna was very upset, and that evening in bed she pressed her face hard into the cushions to stop the tears, until she suddenly heard movements in the spare room. With a leap Joanna was out of bed. Could it be . . . She crept into the passage, listened at the spare room door and opened it very quietly.

She got a dreadful fright: there was Father Christmas! Father Christmas himself, in his red coat and with his red hood on his head. He was standing in front of the looking-glass, combing his beard.

Joanna's mouth fell open. 'Father—' she was about to gasp, but suddenly her arm was jerked, she was pulled back into the passage and the door was closed. It was her mother.

'Oh Joanna, you're not supposed to look. I mean: you mustn't disturb Father Christmas. You must stay in bed and sleep.'

'Yes, but Mummy . . .'

It was no good. Joanna was tucked in again and soon afterwards she heard Father Christmas going out. Bang went the front door.

But I *did* see him, thought Joanna. I know he's true now and I know he's really staying with us.

'Ha, ha,' cried Billy next morning. 'I don't believe it. You're making it up.'

'I'm not.'

'You are.'

'I'm not.'

None of the children believed it except Sylvia, and of course she was Joanna's best friend. 'Do you know what?' said Sylvia. 'We'll come and pick you up to play tomorrow morning. It's Christmas Eve tomorrow and Father Christmas is sure to be there. He'll be having breakfast with you and we'll be able to see him for ourselves.'

Sylvia always had good ideas.

But Mummy looked thoughtful. 'I don't know if Father Christmas . . .' she began hesitantly, but suddenly Daddy said:

'I think he would. He'll need a good breakfast before he starts work, so he won't be leaving too early.'

Joanna was so excited that it took her a long time to get to sleep that night and her mother had to call her three times next morning. 'Father Christmas is having breakfast,' her mother called.

Am I dreaming? thought Joanna.

When she came down to the dining room at last,

Sylvia and Maria and Billy and Ann and Jeremy and Martin and Freddie were there and . . . at the table, calmly spreading his toast, was Father Christmas. He actually had a little egg caught on his beard.

'How late you are, Joanna,' said Father Christmas. 'Come and sit down quickly.'

Joanna pinched herself to see if she was not dreaming after all. But Father Christmas was really there. He drank a cup of tea and ate another slice of toast and marmalade and all the children who had come, full of curiosity, to pick Joanna up, stood round watching him.

'Yes,' said Father Christmas. 'You wouldn't believe it, would you? But Joanna was right. She really had seen my box of clothes and where Father Christmas's clothes are, Father Christmas himself is not far away.'

# Snowy

SHEILA LAVELLE

It was Emma who heard the dog on the roof on Christmas morning, after dreaming of sleighbells jingling and reindeer's hoofbeats in the snow. She woke up in her room in the attic, and at first she couldn't believe her ears.

She sat up and listened. Then she heard it again and she knew she was right. She ran along the landing to her sister's room.

'Katie, wake up,' she said, shaking her shoulder. 'There's a dog on the roof.'

Katie groaned and pulled her pillow over her head.

'Don't be stupid, Emma,' she said. 'How could there be?'

There was more barking and yelping from just above their heads, and Emma dashed back to her room.

She stood on the bed and unfastened the catch on the skylight window, banging upwards on the frame. A blast of air made her hair stand on end as the window flew open and let in the cold December morning.

Emma stuck her head outside. Snow was falling fast, and a thick covering lay on the roof and on the roofs of the houses all around.

Then Emma saw something strange. Here and there on the roof, quickly disappearing under fresh flakes, were footprints in the snow.

Emma stared, remembering her dream. The footprints looked as if they had been made by a large pair of wellies, and there were others that could have been the prints of hooves. There were even some long, deep grooves that looked a bit like the skidmarks from the runners of a sleigh. Don't be stupid, Emma, said Emma to herself, and blinked the snow out of her eyes.

The barking began again, and it was then that Emma saw the small white shape beside the chimney pot.

'Katie, it is a dog,' she called. 'Come and see.'

The dog pricked up his ears at the sound of Emma's voice. He stared at her hopefully, then threw back his head and howled at the sky.

'Good grief,' said Katie, appearing in Emma's door-way. 'How did it get up there?' She pushed Emma out of the way and stuck her head outside.

'Go and get Mum and Gran,' she said, after staring for a moment. 'We'll have to get him down.'

It was the strangest Christmas morning Emma had ever had. What with Mum climbing out on the roof in her dressing-gown and almost falling off, and what with the excitement of getting the dog down at last by tempting him with a cold sausage, and what with all the arguments about how the dog had got there and who he belonged to and what they were going to do with him—Emma even forgot to open her presents.

'Go and look in the front room,' said Gran, as Emma and Katie rubbed the dog with a towel and gave him some milk. 'You haven't seen what Father Christmas has brought you.'

Katie laughed. 'There's no such person as Father Christmas,' she said scornfully, but she ran with Emma to unwrap the pile of parcels under the Christmas tree all the same.

After breakfast Mum phoned the police. 'Nobody has reported a dog missing,' she said when she came back into the kitchen. 'I said we'd keep him here until he's claimed. He seems a nice little dog now that he's dry. What shall we call him?'

Emma looked at the dog's fluffy coat. 'He looks like an Eskimo dog,' she said. 'Let's call him Snowy, because we found him in the snow.' And even Katie agreed that it was a good idea.

What nobody could agree about was how the dog came to be on the roof in the first place. There was no way he could have climbed up there by himself.

Katie said he must have fallen out of an aeroplane, but that didn't seem likely. Gran thought he must have come down by parachute, but as there was no parachute, that didn't seem possible either. Mum thought he must have been put there by somebody having a joke, but Emma didn't think it was a very funny joke. All day she kept thinking of her dream, and of the sleighbells, and of those strange footprints in the snow.

Nobody came forward to claim him, and Snowy became Emma's dog. He followed her everywhere, and he slept on her bed in the attic, although Mum didn't altogether approve. Emma took him for walks every day after school, she fed him and brushed him, and she saved up her pocket money to buy him a collar and lead.

When summer came Emma took Snowy for picnics by the river, and he even went with the family for a holiday by the sea, although he didn't seem to like hot weather, and spent most of his time looking for somewhere cool to lie down.

'He is a funny dog,' said Gran one day. 'He keeps trying to curl up in the fridge!'

'He likes cold places,' said Emma. 'Perhaps he comes from the North Pole.'

'Don't be stupid, Emma,' said Gran. 'There aren't any dogs at the North Pole. Only polar bears.'

Emma said nothing more, but she gave Snowy an ice-cube to lick whenever she got the chance.

Snowy was well looked after and had everything a dog could wish for, but he never completely settled down. Emma would watch him sometimes as he lay in the garden with his nose on his paws, gazing up at the sky, and she knew that he would never be happy in his new home. He seemed to be waiting for something, or for somebody. Emma would look at his sad brown eyes and wish that she could help.

Autumn came, and then winter. Snowy became more and more restless as Christmas came round once again. He spent more and more time in the attic, sitting on Emma's bed, watching the sky through the skylight window.

On Christmas Eve it began to snow.

'Whatever's the matter with that dog?' said Mum, shooing him off the bed for the hundredth time. 'He keeps gazing into the sky. I can't imagine why.'

'He wants to get out on the roof,' said Emma.

'Don't be stupid, Emma,' said Mum. 'What would he want to do that for?'

When Emma went to bed she lay in the dark for a long time, stroking the dog's ears and thinking. If she was right about Snowy, there was only one thing to do. And tonight was the only night she could do it.

Emma thought and thought, and at last she finally made up her mind. She propped herself up against the pillows, determined to stay awake all night.

It was Snowy's whining that woke her a few hours later, from a dream of sleighbells jingling and reindeer's hoofbeats in the snow.

Emma sat up and listened.

She hadn't been dreaming.

Real sleighbells were jingling, real hooves were clip-clopping, and somebody in big wellies was stamping about on the roof above Emma's head.

Snowy went wild. He jumped up at the skylight, yelping and wagging his tail.

Emma knew she had no time to waste. She stood up on the bed and flung the window open, letting in a gust

of cold wind and a flurry of snow. She picked Snowy up in her arms and hugged him tightly to her for a moment.

'Goodbye, Snowy,' she said into his fur, and bundled him out onto the roof. With a quick lick at her face the dog was gone.

Emma heard Snowy barking, and then she heard something else that made her shiver with excitement in her pyjamas.

'So that's where you are!' said a deep voice that made Emma think of plum pudding and mince pies. 'Did you fall off the sleigh? We'd better make sure that doesn't happen again, hadn't we?'

Hooves drummed on the roof, there was a sudden jingling of bells and then silence. Emma closed the window and went back to bed.

She knew she would miss Snowy, but that didn't matter. What mattered was that he was on his way home.

There was a big fuss the next morning as everybody looked for Snowy. Mum, Gran and Katie searched the house from top to bottom, calling his name. Mum even reported it to the police.

'What can have happened to him?' she said. 'Do you know anything, Emma? You don't seem very upset.'

Emma only shook her head and said nothing. It wasn't worth telling anybody anything. She knew exactly what they would all say.

# Really, Truly, Reilly

ANNE MERRICK

On the night before Christmas the weather was cold and Samuel Shrubwort came home from work in a terrible temper.

When they heard him snarling through the hall, Oscar the cat, flimsy as a shadow, fled upstairs while Reilly, the small white dog with one black eye and one brown, slunk out of sight beneath the table.

'Scram!' bawled Samuel Shrubwort, giving the table a kick. 'Get out, you HORRIBLE, SCRAWNY, USELESS dog!'

*Useless?* thought Reilly. *Who's he calling useless? It's starving I am. Cold and uncared for as a long-buried bone. Really and truly, this is no life for a dog!*

And seizing his chance while Samuel Shrubwort drank another tankard of beer, Reilly squeezed through Oscar's cat-flap and escaped into the stone-cold winter street.

The weather was so cold that the stars were shivering in the sky; so cold that all the trees turned white with frost and stood about the gardens like bony ghosts of themselves; so cold that in every house in Hometown, the fires burned with a blue flame.

But from the Great Hall on the hilltop to the Small Shack by the river, all the windows of the village beamed with warm and friendly light.

*Heigh-ho,* said Reilly. *On the night before Christmas, surely someone will give a home to a small white dog with one black eye and one brown.*

And after a moment's thought he trotted up the hill to the Great Hall where the rich man lived.

On the night before Christmas, the rich man was counting his gold when he heard a sniffing and a scratching at his door.

'Help!' he cried. 'Thieves! Robbers! Burglars! Bandits!'

*R-r-really!* growled Reilly. *I am not a BANDIT! I'm just a small white dog with one black eye and one brown, and if you give me a home I'll guard your gold for you!*

'Be off!' shouted the rich man. 'Or I'll call the POLICE!'

Then he drew the bolt across the door and the curtains across the window, shutting off the warm and friendly light.

*Talk about giving a dog a bad name!* thought Reilly. *Really and truly I wouldn't want to live there anyway.*

But he had a lonely kind of feeling inside as he

started back down the hill, trying each house as he went.

To the man in the Church House he protested, *I am* NOT *the* DEVIL HIMSELF. *I'm just a dog-in-need. A lonely kind of a dog. And if you give me a home I'll do good works for you.*

To the lady in the Pretty Pink Cottage, he pleaded, *But I am* NOT A MANGY OLD FLEA-BAG! *I'm just a lonely dog. A useful kind of a dog. And I'll fetch your slippers for you if you'll only give me a home.*

To the farmer in the Farmhouse, he barked, *What!* WORRY YOUR SHEEP! *Never! I'm just a dogged kind of a dog. A lonely, useful dog. And if you give me a home, I'll work my whiskers off for you!*

And to the inn-keeper at the Welcome Inn, he howled, *Oh no I'm* NOT A PESKY SCAVENGING STRAY. *I'm just a dog-in-need. A dogged dog. A lonely, useful kind of a dog. Really and truly I'm used to drunks! I'll chivvy them out and chase them home, if only you'll give me a bed and a bone!*

On the night before Christmas, by the time Reilly had gone all the way down the hill, the curtains of every house in Hometown were closed. Only in the Small Shack by the river a feeble candle flame still flickered.

Reilly limped to the Shack and sat on the doorstep. His paws were so caked with ice that he could not lift them to scratch at the door.

*Heigh-ho!* he sighed. *Here I am, a small white dog with one black eye and one brown. A dog-in-need. A dogged dog. But there's nobody in this world who will give me a home!* And in spite of himself two tears rolled down his muzzle and froze into pearls on his whiskers.

*Perhaps after all,* he cried, *I'm a* HORRIBLE . . . SCRAWNY . . . USELESS . . . *kind of a dog. A lonely, home-less dog.*

Early on the morning of Christmas Day it snowed and soon all the houses of Hometown lay snug under a dazzling white quilt. Inside the Small Shack by the river Tim Merryweather stoked up the fire and he, his wife Lovejoy, and Jo-John their son, sat close around it. From a pot on the hob a warm smell of onion soup wafted up to the rafters.

Tim Merryweather began to play the fiddle. He played the tunes of his favourite carols while Lovejoy sang the words. And on a patchwork blanket by the hearth, Jo-John stroked the head of a small white dog with one black eye and one brown.

'Tell me again,' said Jo-John, 'how he came to be my Christmas present—when I wasn't going to *have* any present . . .'

So Tim Merryweather rested his fiddle on his knee and told how he'd just been saying his bedtime prayers when he'd heard a small sad cry outside.

'And when I opened the door,' he said, 'I darn near fell over him. Frozen to the step he was! Dog-tired and nearly done for!'

Lovejoy stirred the pot of onion soup.

'It seems to me,' she laughed, 'he must be a holy kind of a dog. Coming like that in answer to our prayers!'

Then Jo-John took from his pocket a morsel of the sausage he'd had for his breakfast and popped it into Reilly's grinning mouth.

'He's going to be my very best friend,' he said. 'My one and only dog in the world!'

On the morning of Christmas Day, the small white dog with one black eye and one brown swallowed the sausage in one gulp.

*Really and truly,* he said, *this is the life! And to think that only yesterday I was a horrible, useless, wholly lonely dog. And today I am the one-and-only-HOLY-kind-of-a-dog-in-the-world!*

And licking Jo-John's hand for the very last taste of the sausage, he winked his one black eye.

# The Christmas Cake

JOHN GORDON

Nisha had nothing to do. She had played with all her toys, Christmas dinner was over, and now it was dark outside and everyone in the house seemed to be asleep. 'Except me,' said Nisha to herself, and she wandered into the room where the big table was already laid for tea.

The room was full of shadows because the only light came from the Christmas tree in the corner, and it was so quiet she could very nearly hear the tinsel glittering on its branches.

114

Nisha had helped her mother, Sally, to put the icing on the Christmas cake. Then she and her father, Vidya, had decorated the top, making a snow scene that had a snowman and carol-singers, and a forest of little trees which she had picked out of the decorations box and stuck into the white icing. Now it stood in the middle of the table, with the tea-cups set out around it and a cracker beside each plate. Nisha went up close to one of the crackers and peeped into its open end. There was a little man inside singing carols.

'I wish you a merry Christmas,' he sang, 'I wish you a merry Christmas . . .' and then he turned his head and saw her.

'I've been waiting for you for ages,' he said. 'Hurry up.' So she stepped inside and walked along the paper tunnel, looking at the paper walls and the paper ceiling

until she tripped over something and fell down flat on the paper floor.

'I see you are just as clumsy as ever,' said the man. 'Why did you do that?'

'I couldn't help it,' said Nisha, and looked down at the big paper bundle that had tripped her up. 'What is it, anyway?'

'Haven't you ever been inside a cracker before?' he said.

'No,' she said, rubbing her knee. 'Have you?'

'Of course I have,' said the little man. 'They don't call me Crackerjack for nothing.' He gave the bundle a kick. 'Anyone can see what that is. It's a paper hat.'

And then Nisha saw that the bundle had a huge elastic band around it. 'It must be for a very big head,' she said.

'Yours, I expect.' That made him chuckle, but Nisha's head was no longer very big, because she was small enough to be inside a cracker.

'Why do you want to see me?' she asked.

'That's obvious,' snapped Crackerjack. 'You've got to help me find my way through the forest.'

'What forest?' said Nisha.

'Stop arguing,' he said impatiently, 'and follow me.'

They clambered out of the end of the cracker and stood on the tablecloth. It was quite dark, but she could just make out that Crackerjack had a top hat, a long green coat, and a yellow scarf. She thought she might have seen him somewhere before, but his top hat had a bend in it and she didn't remember that.

'It's getting darker,' said Crackerjack. 'Pity we haven't got a candle.'

'There are some candles on the cake,' said Nisha, 'but nobody has been able to light them because we can't find any matches.' Sally and Vidya had searched high and low, but there wasn't a single match in the house. And now Nisha stood by the cake and it towered over her like a mountain.

Crackerjack tilted his head as if he was trying to catch sight of something high overhead. 'Can't see a thing,' he said crossly. 'Pity about those matches.' And then he put both hands beside his mouth and shouted upwards, 'Hello, up there! Have you gone to sleep!' He shuffled his feet and grumbled, 'Blooming snowmen—they always keep you waiting.'

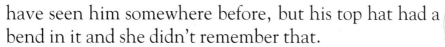

'I can't see any snowmen,' said Nisha.

'You will if you can afford to wait long enough,' he grumbled.

The paper cake band rose above them like a great wall of red. 'We've got to get to the top of this cliff somehow,' he said, and once again he cupped his hands and shouted up, 'Wake up, Bill! Stir your stumps!'

And then, very slowly, the red frill at the top was pushed aside and a round face with a very wide grin looked down at them. It was a snowman.

'You're too slow to catch a cold, Bill,' said Cracker-jack.

'I don't have to catch one,' said Bill, 'because I'm cold all the time.' His grin became so wide that his

118

little eyes were screwed up and almost disappeared.

Crackerjack hugged himself to keep warm. 'My feet are like ice,' he said.

'So are mine,' said the snowman, and he thought that was even funnier.

'When you've quite finished enjoying yourself,' snapped Crackerjack, 'you can unwind your scarf and throw one end down to us.'

'Righty-ho,' said Bill. 'Won't take a jiffy.'

'A likely story,' said Crackerjack, but in no time the end of Bill's scarf came snaking down the red cliff, and they both clung to it while Bill hauled them up.

Crackerjack shivered. 'It's freezing up here,' he said, and wherever Nisha looked there was nothing but white snow.

'It's snow use complaining,' said Bill. 'Snow use at all,' and he was chuckling so much his little black eyes vanished completely so that only his smile remained. It was then that Nisha recognized him.

'I know who you are, Bill,' she said, because she had made him out of marzipan and covered him with icing sugar before she put him on the cake—and suddenly she remembered where she had seen Crackerjack. He was one of the carol-singers she had taken out of the decorations box and put on the snow near the house. All the carol-singers were little figures that had come from crackers.

'Crackerjack,' she said, looking at him, 'why aren't you with the other carol-singers?'

'Because you dropped me and bent my hat,' he snapped.

'I'm sorry,' she said, and felt a tear rolling down her cheek.

'When you've dried those big dark eyes,' said Crackerjack, 'we'll get on,' and he and Bill leant over and patted her cheeks dry with their scarves.

'Now we'll have to hurry,' said Crackerjack, 'or they'll start the carols without me.'

Nisha walked between them, but now that she was so small the snow seemed to stretch away for ever and she wished she hadn't made it so bumpy when she'd put the icing on the cake.

'Halt!' said Crackerjack, because they had come to

the edge of a forest. 'It is dark and dangerous in there, so we need someone to show us the way,' and he looked at Nisha.

'But I've never been here before,' she said.

'Is that so?' He didn't seem to believe her. 'May I ask who it was who planted this forest?'

'Oh,' said Nisha, because now she remembered taking the spiky, dark green trees out of the decorations box and sticking them in the icing. 'But I never knew I was going to have to go into the forest,' she said.

'And there's a monster in there,' said Crackerjack.

'I don't like monsters,' said Bill, and he began to shiver so much that one of the silver buttons that Nisha had stuck on his front fell off. She picked it up, but now the little silver ball was as big as her hand. 'You keep it,' said Bill, 'I'd only shiver it off again.'

Nisha led the way into the forest. She was certain that it had grown bigger than when she'd planted it, and it became darker and darker as they walked. The tree trunks made a long, dim corridor that stretched away into the distance, and far away she could see the glimmer of the open snow. But something stood there, waiting.

'It's the monster!' cried Crackerjack, and quick as a flash he hid behind a tree.

Bill the Snowman was much slower, and anyway he was too fat to hide anywhere, so he stood where he was. 'The monster will eat me first,' he said to Nisha. 'So you'd better run away quick.'

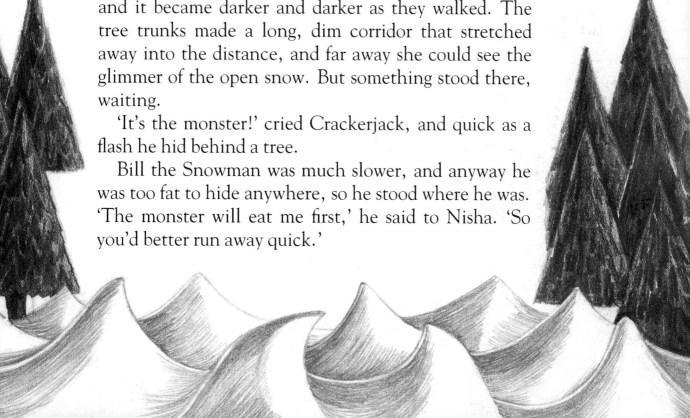

But Nisha knew quite a lot about the top of that Christmas cake, so instead of hiding she walked on.

'Come back!' shouted Bill.

'Come back!' yelled Crackerjack, but Nisha kept on walking.

The monster's huge eyes gazed straight at her, and Nisha heard the voices of Bill and Crackerjack growing fainter and fainter behind her, and suddenly she didn't feel quite so brave. The eyes were very large in a very big head. 'But I'm sure I'm right,' she said to herself, 'I'm quite sure I'm right—at least I hope I'm right,' and she walked right up to the monster and stood in front of it.

The enormous eyes blinked at her, and she said, 'Hello, Robin.'

The robin redbreast was perched on its log exactly where she had placed it, but now it was as big as herself. She held out her hand, and when Crackerjack saw the robin peck the silver button he came forward.

'Nasty things, robins,' he said, pretending to be brave as he and Bill came out of the trees. The robin blinked as they went by.

Now Nisha could see the little house in the distance. She pointed to it and said, 'that's where we'll find the carol-singers.'

They trudged on, and soon they were walking through what Bill thought was a new sort of forest—'if it is a forest,' he said, because all the tree-trunks were straight and crinkled and had no branches.

Nisha looked up. 'These aren't trees, Bill,' she said. 'They're candles.' She had put them there herself, pink and green and blue. 'But I'm afraid they'll never get lit today because we haven't got anything to light them.'

'That's a pity,' said Bill, 'because I should really like to see them all lit up.'

'So should I,' said Nisha, but at that moment the carol-singers all began to sing and Crackerjack went over to join them. They stood in a ring around a lantern on a pole, but Crackerjack marched straight into the middle and picked up the pole and came marching back with all the singers behind him.

They watched him as he went striding towards one of the high candles, opened the little window in his lantern, then lifted it on its pole and touched it to the candle-wick.

'Let's have some light on the subject,' he said, and when the candle flame was standing up like a white almond, he stuck his lantern pole in the snow so that everybody could join hands and dance around it, while their shadows danced with them on the snow.

Suddenly there was the sound of a bell a long way off and everybody stood stock-still, gazing at each other with frightened eyes. Only Nisha knew what it was. It was the front doorbell, and soon all her aunties and uncles and cousins would be in the room.

'It's tea time,' she said.

'What?' cried Crackerjack. 'So soon? Get back to your places everyone!'

People seemed to scatter in every direction, and Nisha found herself holding Bill's hand and running as fast as she could towards the edge of the cake.

'This is where you put me,' said Bill, and dug his feet into the snow, but Nisha slipped and went rolling down the slope faster and faster until she flew over the edge and went tumbling down the red cliff.

She shut her eyes and heard a bump but didn't feel anything. The bump must have been the front door closing, so Nisha opened her eyes.

124

She was still looking into the end of the cracker, trying to see what was inside, but a moment later the room was full of people. Her mother came in and saw the candle burning on the cake. 'Oh, so someone has found some matches after all,' she said, but Nisha looked for the little man and his lantern.

Crackerjack was back among the carol-singers with his head flung back and his mouth wide open. And then she saw the snowman standing beside the forest. 'Hello, Bill,' she whispered, and one of his little black eyes winked and his smile grew wider, but nobody else saw it.

# The Christmas Surprise

MARILYN WATTS

Robert's parents had a surprise for him, they said. Well, it was nearly Christmas and that was the best time for surprises. But for Robert this surprise turned out to be a horrible shock.

It was a cold winter's afternoon, with a cosy fire in the front room, and Robert's little sister Wendy was playing on the rug as usual. Everything was normal, until his mother began to talk about people being lonely at Christmas-time and then went on:

'So, you see, we've invited old Mrs Manley over for Christmas dinner . . .'

Robert stared at her in horror.

'. . . so that she won't be on her own this year,' she went on. 'We thought it would be nice.'

Robert tried looking at his father, but he was smiling in agreement and Robert soon realized it was not going

128

to be any use. Dad was obviously just as determined to wreck their day.

'No!' Robert shouted. 'I don't want her. It'll spoil everything.'

'I don't want her, either,' said Wendy.

Robert was glad that she backed him up. But it didn't do any good. Old Mrs Manley was coming to their house at two o'clock on Christmas Day afternoon, and that was that.

On Christmas Day morning, they opened all the family presents as usual. But it wasn't the same. Mum and Dad disappeared into the kitchen. Wendy played with her new skittles game, swinging the weight round and round to see how many skittles she could knock over in one go. Robert kept watching the clock. It crept round to twelve o'clock, then half-past twelve and one o'clock. By half-past one, Robert had made up his mind that this was going to be the worst Christmas ever. Mum had said he was being selfish, and perhaps he was. But this year it wouldn't be a 'family Christmas'. Robert admitted—to himself—that they did sometimes get on each other's nerves by the end of Christmas Day, and ended up arguing over silly little things. But having old Mrs Manley there wouldn't help; it would just make it a hundred times worse.

The strange thing was, old Mrs Manley didn't seem at all happy when she arrived, either. In fact, she seemed very fed up. Nothing was right for her.

When she saw the front room decorations, she sniffed and said, 'We never had an artificial tree at home.'

When Wendy asked for another mince-pie at dinner, she said, 'You've had two helpings already.'

When she was given a cup of tea after dinner, she asked, 'How many tea-bags did you put in this tea?' And she peered into her cup as though they were trying to poison her.

Old Mrs Manley couldn't get comfortable in the chair they had got ready for her with extra cushions. The room was too hot, she said, and she had forgotten to bring her reading-glasses.

When Mrs Manley had finished her cup of tea, Wendy gave her some little presents. Mum had bought them, and Wendy had wrapped them up and written 'To Mrs Manley' on the labels in her best handwriting. But Mrs Manley just nodded, and grunted, and pushed her lips together into a tight line until they lost all their pink colour. Robert's mother and father looked at each other with raised eyebrows. Wendy was upset and went off, back to her new game. 'So there!' thought Robert. He knew he had been right all along.

Finally, Mrs Manley inched herself out of the chair with extra cushions and stood up.

'Thank you for having me, Mr and Mrs Turner,' she said. 'It's been very nice. But I think I'd better be getting along now.'

'Well, yes,' said Robert's father. 'I'll fetch . . .'

He was interrupted by a long, loud wail from the corner of the room.

'It's broken. It's broken!' screamed Wendy. The weight that was supposed to knock the skittles down had snapped off from its pole, and she was holding the broken clasp in her hand.

'Oh, Wendy,' said her father, 'you've only just got it.'

'I didn't mean to,' said Wendy. She held out the small bit of plastic as though someone in the room could work miracles.

Someone could.

'We used to have that game when I was your age,' said Mrs Manley suddenly. 'But not plastic. Have you got some string? And you need something small and heavy.'

'Marbles?' asked Robert.

'They'll do. Do you still have them nowadays?'

'Of course,' he said. And went to get some.

'How did you play it?' Wendy asked.

Old Mrs Manley didn't look so old as she worked, twisting the string into a sack for the marbles and showing Wendy how to tie it to the top of the pole. And while her fingers mended the game, her voice conjured up Christmases long gone. She told them the story of her Aunt Joanna and the New Year kitten. And while they played skittles together she told them about her brother Herbert, when he was young, and what happened when he tried to sail his new model battleship on the park pond even though it was all frozen over.

'. . . so we were sent to bed very early,' she finished. 'But our clothes were frozen solid and didn't dry for two whole days.'

Robert and Wendy laughed. Robert tried to imagine it but couldn't. They had a tumble-dryer.

Mrs Manley smiled at her memories.

Wendy had decided by now that Mrs Manley was winning too often at her skittles game. 'What else did you and your brother play?' she asked.

Mrs Manley thought for a minute. 'Well,' she said, 'the best game we ever invented was called "Chase the Elephant".'

'How do you play it?' asked Robert.

It was a *very* good game. After a few minutes, their father put his head round the door to see what all the noise was about. He found Robert stretched out on the table and Wendy crawling underneath it making the weirdest noises. Then Mrs Manley clapped her hands and called out 'rhinoceros'. Mr Turner was only just able to close the door in time as Robert jumped off the table and started shouting 'Nellie, Nellie', while Wendy scuttled out from under the table and ran in the opposite direction. Mr and Mrs Turner decided it was safer to stay in the kitchen.

Later, Robert came into the kitchen to ask if they could have something to drink.

'I'm not surprised, with all that yelling going on,' said his father. 'I'll make some squash. There's cake, too.'

'Having a good time?' his mother asked.

'Great!' Robert grinned. He picked up a piece of Christmas cake and bit into it, thoughtfully. Then he said, 'She wasn't very good fun to start with, though.'

'I think she was too proud to admit she needed us,' said Robert's father.

Robert looked at him, and remembered the boring Christmases.

'But we needed her!' he said. And ran off.

# White Christmas

NINA BEACHCROFT

'Christmas is coming,' people were saying at Rushida's school.

'What's the *best* thing about Christmas?' Rushida asked her friend Jane.

'Presents,' said Jane immediately. 'You get lots of presents. And good things to eat—roast turkey and Christmas pudding.'

'I don't know if we'll have that,' said Rushida doubtfully. 'What else happens?'

'Parties happen,' said Jane. 'And there's the Nativity play the Infants are doing—you'll see it next week. It's all about Jesus being born in a stable.'

135

Rushida and Jane were first year Juniors. They felt much older than the Infants, whose classrooms were in a different part of the school buildings.

'I was an angel last year in the play, before you came,' Jane said dreamily, remembering. 'It was because I'm fair. I look like an angel, see? Me and Sharon and Mandy and Denise, we were all angels. We had wings. One of mine fell off, I was all lop-sided! You'd have laughed. And *you* were funny too, when you couldn't speak any English. But I liked you.'

Rushida giggled at the memory too. She and her family had come to England from Bangladesh at the end of February. She remembered how cold she had felt. She remembered many, many things.

'I wanted to ask you how you could see out of your blue eyes,' she told Jane. 'I hadn't seen blue or green eyes before England. I thought perhaps the people who had them were blind.'

'Blind! Don't be silly!' cried Jane. She began to wrestle with Rushida, both of them laughing, until Miss Robinson, their form teacher, stopped them.

'You two,' she said, 'one so dark and the other so fair, but you've a lot in common. You're both a couple of tomboys.'

'What's tomboys, then?' asked Rushida.

'Girls who are better than boys!' cried Jane. 'Girls who like cars and aeroplanes just as much as dolls.'

'Come on, everybody, sit down,' said Miss Robinson to the whole class. 'I'm going to read you a story about

Christmas. It'll be here soon. Anybody done some Christmas shopping yet?'

Some of the children answered her, but Rushida kept silent. She knew that Christmas was going to be another of those things that weren't the same for Muslim families, such as her own. Her family had festivals to celebrate, but they were different ones. Early last summer, there had been Eid, coming after the month's fast of Ramadan. For all that time the grown-ups in her family had eaten and drunk nothing between the hours of sunrise and sunset: their religion had forbidden it. When it was all over, there had been a big party with lots of good food, and she and her older sister, and her nine-year old brother, Ahmed, and her two-year old baby brother had all had new clothes.

The story that Miss Robinson was reading out loud was called 'White Christmas' and it was about snow coming on Christmas Day, and changing the world. Rushida listened with her mouth open. She had heard of snow before, but never seen it. How she longed to see it and find out what it was really like!

When she got home that afternoon she asked her cousin Hassan about snow. Hassan had been in England with his parents and his older brothers since he was five, and now he was twelve. They all lived in the top half of Rushida's house. Hassan's father and Rushida's father were brothers.

'Snow is like ice-cream. It comes from the sky and covers the whole world, and you can eat it, only you mustn't eat too much, because then all your insides freeze and you turn into a snowman,' said Hassan, his eyes glinting.

'I don't believe you,' said Rushida, with dignity.

'You can pick it up and throw it in balls,' said Hassan.

'Maybe,' thought Rushida. 'Maybe not.' Hassan liked teasing her, that she did know.

'There's a model of Father Christmas in a shop in the High Street,' said her brother Ahmed then. 'He has a white beard, and he's driving a cart on snow. Haven't you seen him yet? You're stupid, you don't know anything.'

'Not a cart, a sledge,' corrected Hassan. 'Drawn by reindeer. And he has a sack full of presents. He's supposed to come down people's chimneys and give out the presents.'

'You're having me on,' said Rushida, using the English words, and Hassan just laughed.

Christmas Day came at last, and to Rushida's disappointment it was a day like any other, cold, and raining a little.

'I hate English rain,' thought Rushida, as she pressed her face to the window. 'I hate grey streets, and cars. I want to be back in the village in Bangladesh. I want to run in the fields after the rice harvest, when they are all golden and empty. When the rains come, I want to skim along the water in a boat. I want to see all the relations we left behind . . . I want to see the ducks and the chickens and the goats and our cow . . . the water buffalo with his beautiful curving horns that our uncle owns . . . I want to wade into our pond again, under the heat of the sun, and sit on the steps and dry, oh, so quickly. . . .'

She had been quite happy in England for months, but now she wept.

'I hate Christmas,' she said to Ahmed.

'You're just stupid,' he told her. 'Christmas is for Western people, anyway.'

The next day was called Boxing Day. What a funny name that was! There was an odd feel to the air, and a kind of quietness, as Rushida got out of bed.

'Look out of the window!' Ahmed shouted.

Outside, the world was white. Something white lay thickly in their garden, covering the grass, so that no green showed. It lay on the walls and on the bare branches of the trees; each twig had its covering.

'Snow!' they shouted. They all dressed as quickly as possible, and rushed outside, even the grown-ups.

They scooped up the snow and threw it, and Ahmed even rolled in it. It tasted of cold water, not ice-cream. It stung the lips and cheeks and hands, it was so cold.

Soon the toddler was crying, and Ahmed was moaning, 'Ow, the snow hurts. It's got down my back! Ugh!'

They ran in to find dry clothes and to warm themselves, and Rushida looked back at the garden that had been so fresh and white, sparkling in the sun like diamonds.

It was all trampled and messed up, and she felt like weeping again. Why couldn't the snow have lasted? In the road outside, cars came swishing along, and the snow was dirty and churned up.

140

But while they were eating their midday meal; large, soft snowflakes began to drift down from the sky; it grew dark and heavy looking, and the snow fell on and on, quietening the world again.

At last, well into the afternoon, the flakes stopped falling, and their back garden was new.

'I shall make a snowman,' cried Hassan. 'Ahmed, you can help.'

'I shall help too,' said Rushida.

'No, this is man's work. You're a girl.'

'So what? I shall make something else,' cried Rushida.

She put on heavy gloves and collected deep armfuls of snow, piling it up so it looked like a . . . It looked like a . . .

Why, from above it looked like a big bird, an eagle, its wings half outstretched! She carefully added to one wing, smoothed the other. Now the head. She shaped a knob of snow like a bird's head, cut away snow underneath to shape the body. After much searching, she found a bent twig to be the eagle's beak, little stones for the eyes . . .

141

*Yes*, there was her eagle looking at her, a truly magic bird. She could fly back to the village on him. He would take her wherever she wished.

'Yah!' shouted Ahmed. He was cold and cross, because Hassan had been ordering him about over their snowman.

He kicked at Rushida's bird. Fumf! The wings lost their shape, the beak and eyes disappeared.

The magic bird was just a heap of snow again.

Rushida ran inside the house and buried her face in the sofa cushions. She stayed there a long time.

'My beautiful bird, all gone,' she thought. 'Nothing lasts. I shall never see the village again.'

Suddenly there was a knock on the front door. It was her friend Jane, who lived near.

'I've got a Christmas present for Rushida,' said Jane. 'I couldn't bring it yesterday, we were out all day.'

She handed Rushida a parcel, wrapped in shiny Christmas paper. Inside was a gleaming aeroplane, about six inches long, with blue body and silver wings. It had a propeller, and wheels that whirred round.

'I want one too,' said Ahmed enviously.

'No. It's *my* Christmas present,' cried Rushida fiercely, 'given me by my friend. A good friend is better than a bad brother! She has changed my bird into an aeroplane. That means one day I will fly wherever I like. Oh, I think Christmas is really great, now!'

'And next Christmas,' said the practical Jane, '*you* can give *me* a present.'

# Wil's Tail

## HAZEL HUTCHINS

Wilmot James Edward Hutchins was the sixth wolf from the left at the school Christmas Concert. When the concert was over everyone said what a good Christmas forest creature he'd been and everyone admired his costume. Wil admired his costume too—especially the tail.

It was a wonderful tail. His mother had made it from the belt of her old fake-fur coat. Wil himself had sewed it to the seat of his favourite corduroy trousers. It was the kind of a tail that hung 'just right' and swung 'just right'. It was the kind of a tail with which Wil could slink or jump; the kind of a tail he could twirl or drape; the kind of a tail he could curl smoothly around him. It had patterns and lines and colours in it that Wil had never even thought about before, and it was softer than anything he'd ever known.

When Wil got home, he hung the wolf mask on his bedroom wall. He put the sweater (his Dad's) back in the big dresser drawer. He put the mittens (his sister's) and the moccasins (his mother's) back in the closet where they belonged. But he kept the tail.

The next day was Christmas Eve. Wil helped wrap presents and eat biscuits. When evening came, his family went to a party at the neighbours. Wil's Dad wore his smart jeans. Wil's Mum wore her party blouse. Wil's sister wore sixteen hair-slides. And Wil wore his tail.

He wore it during supper and he wore it during games and he wore it during carol-singing. The neighbours thought it a bit strange, but they were too polite to say anything.

Wil was tired when he got home. He hung up his stocking and rolled into bed. His tail rolled into bed too, all except the tip which hung out over the edge.

On Christmas morning, Wil's family hugged and kissed and opened presents and ate breakfast. They went to the cousins for the day. Wil's Dad wore his Christmas tie. Wil's Mum wore her Christmas perfume. Wil's sister wore her Christmas brooch and her Christmas socks. Wil wore his Christmas tail.

Aunt Beth nearly had a heart attack when she stepped on it in the kitchen.

On Boxing Day, the family ate left-overs and played 327 games of draughts. The next day they went shopping in the city. Everyone wore their everyday, ordinary clothes. Wil wore his tail.

145

The tip of it got caught in the escalator of Krumings' department store. A loud warning bell went off. Two security people and three maintenance personnel worked to free the mechanism and every shopper in the whole store came to see the boy whose tail had been caught between the second and third floors.

For the rest of the week Wil stayed at home with his tail. He repaired it with an extra piece, so it was longer than ever. He built a den in the basement. He took long naps in front of the fire with the cat. And he waited for New Year's Eve.

On New Year's Eve the family always went skating on Whitefish Lake. Wil was planning on wearing his tail. He could just see himself streaking down the lake in the darkness; the wind rushing smoothly against his face and his tail flying far out behind.

But when New Year's Eve came and he tried to tuck his tail up under his sweater, his mother looked at him and shook her head.

'No,' she said. 'It's dangerous. You'll trip over it and fall and so will everybody else.'

Wil appealed to his father.

'No,' he said. 'It's dangerous. When you go and warm up at the bonfire you're likely to set yourself ablaze.'

'But it's part of me!' said Wil.

His parents did not agree.

'All right,' said Wil. 'I'll wear it but I won't go skating and I won't go near the fire.'

His parents gave in.

Whitefish Lake on New Year's Eve was wonderful.
People from all over came to skate and laugh and warm
themselves around an enormous bonfire. Wil climbed a
little hill between the lake and the river which flowed
beyond. He listened to the wonderful sound of skate-
blades on ice. He watched skaters passing hockey
pucks, turning figures of eight, and playing tick. Just
when he could stand it no longer and had decided to
take off his tail and put on his skates, he heard shouting
behind him.

'Someone's fallen through the river ice!' called the man.

'We can't reach them. A rope. A long scarf. Help! Anyone, please!' called the woman.

Wil thought for only a moment. He reached behind him and pulled with all his might. With a rip his tail came loose. He raced down the slope. The woman took it without a word and disappeared into the darkness.

Wil never did get to go skating on Whitefish Lake that New Year's Eve. By the time all the excitement died down, it was time for his family to go home.

But he did get his tail back. The woman who'd taken it made a special point of bringing it back to him. It was sodden and torn and about four feet longer than it had been to start with. Wil didn't care. His tail had actually saved someone's life!

The tail sits, these days, curled up in a special place, right in the middle of Wil's bedroom shelf—an heroic Christmas tail.

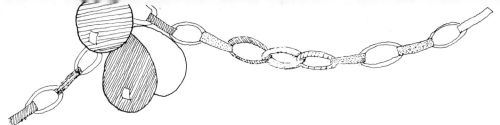

# The Good Witch Befana

RACHEL ANDERSON

Jason, like the coloured paper-chains slung across the classroom, was drooping.

'Boring, boring,' he muttered, loud enough for Ahmed sitting next to him to hear, but not Miss Wright.

Dreary Deirdre droned on about the shiny star on her tree at home as though it was something truly amazing, and they all had to pretend to be interested.

Miss Wright had been working on a special topic all week. 'Festivities in Other Lands', she called it. They'd learned about Mexican children's clay *piñatas* full of sweetmeats, and Australian children eating plum pudding on sunny beaches. They had heard stories about Saint Lucia of Sweden wearing a garland of leaves and four candles on her head to light up the world, and Italian stories about the good witch Befana arriving on her broomstick. Jason wasn't so keen on those. A witch, even an Italian one who brought chocolate to children at Epiphany twelve days after Christmas, was scary.

Now, on the last day of term, Miss Wright was

149

rounding up with a discussion on how people in Britain liked to celebrate. And it sounded as though every family in the Maples End Road would be enjoying the same things—turkey, tree, presents. Even Ahmed, whose parents ought to have known better since they were Muslims, was going to have Christmas presents.

'Makes you sick,' Jason grumbled. 'Presents, presents, presents.'

'What was that, dear?'

'Nothing.' Jason preferred it when Miss Wright didn't notice he was there.

'Ah, Jason. Yes, we'll have your turn now, shall we? Let's hear how you and your father usually spend the holiday.'

Jason wished Miss Wright didn't know about him living just with his Dad. And he certainly didn't want anybody to know about their Christmas plans. The fact was, they weren't going to do anything. Or, as Dad put it, 'We'll not bother much with the fancy stuff this year. You're getting a bit old for all that now, aren't you, son?'

'Well . . .' Jason had begun because he hadn't thought that a person ever got too old for surprises.

Now, wearily, he stood up, took a deep breath and began. 'We'll be going to my rich relatives.'

'Why, that *does* sound exciting,' said Miss Wright, and the class murmured approval, all except Sarah who, so she told everyone, was getting her own video-recorder.

'In Scotland,' Jason added to make it sound good and far away from the Maples End Road School.

Miss Wright, who knew everything, knew all about Scotland too. It seemed that lots of folk up there didn't celebrate on the 25th but saved up for Hogmanay instead. 'That's their New Year,' she explained.

'So Jason won't get any presents, then, will he?' piped up Sarah with a smirk. 'Chose the wrong relatives, didn't he?'

Later, as they undecorated their classroom, Sarah asked Miss if she could have the paper-chains which were being thrown away. Jason wished he'd thought to ask first. Sarah only wanted them for her hamster to chew up, whereas Jason could have used them to decorate the flat. Out in the playground he asked Sarah if she'd go halves. But she just said, 'You haven't got no hamster, stupid.'

When Jason let himself into the flat, it seemed gloomier than usual, especially compared to number 83 opposite, with their fairy lights flashing all round the door.

Jason knew it wasn't *really* that Dad disapproved of trees and tinsel. It was more that he just hadn't the heart. Everything they might have done, Mum had always done so much better, only now she wasn't coming back.

152

D'you know, Mum, he wanted to say, in Poland on Christmas Eve, they let their animals come in and eat at the table! And in Sweden they make a wreath with four candles to remember Saint Lucia. And in Italy— but no, best not to think about that one.

As soon as Dad came home, he pushed a plastic bag into Jason's hands. Football boots, real leather, proper screw-in studs. Jason was dead pleased with them. Though he'd have preferred Dad to have wrapped them in a bit of pretty paper like Mum used to do. No person, Jason considered, could ever get too old to enjoy a surprise.

And that was when he had his good idea. A surprise he could do for Dad that wouldn't remind him of Mum.

Dad was working right up till Christmas Eve, so Jason had plenty of time.

'Be all right then, son? On your own?' asked Dad, worried.

' 'Course I will,' said Jason. For now he had something important to get on with.

Jason hadn't listened that carefully to Miss Wright's 'Festivities in Other Lands', but he did remember some of it. Specially about the Swedish wreath with candles. And the Russian bit about cleaning the house for Christmas. And the French bit about feasting at midnight.

And of course that Italian bit. But as he busied about tidying the flat, Jason made himself forget about the witch Befana. She was spooky and anyway she didn't come till afterwards.

153

After tidying up, he went downstairs to the courtyard where the bins were and picked some twigs off the hedge. Not quite the same as holly and ivy, but good enough to weave into a bushy wreath to go round the candles.

Dad had left the food ready to cook for their tea when he got back. Boring old bacon and boiled potatoes, same as usual. But with a clean cloth on the table, cushions on the two chairs, and a tin of fruit salad, Jason managed to make it look like a proper feast.

Jason could tell by Dad's face when he got in that he was surprised. And pleased.

'Well I never did!' he said.

Dad had two days off, then it was back to work, same as usual. Luckily there was plenty of good stuff on the telly in the holidays.

Jason didn't really like being left by himself all through the days after Christmas. He sometimes used to pretend that his Mum was coming back. But he knew she wouldn't, so there was no point in wishing.

He specially didn't much like it when Dad was on late-shift. It always seemed to grow dark earlier than Jason expected, and there were strange shadows under the doors which weren't there in the daytime. Then Jason couldn't help thinking about that Italian in her long black cloak.

Miss Wright had said how the Befana went creeping around on the twelfth night after Christmas, searching out the good children and the bad. Was he one of the good ones? Or the bad?

It was nearly time for school to start again. He'd have to hear all about Sarah's presents.

Suddenly, there was a soft knock at the front door. Jason pretended to himself he hadn't heard it. But when it came again, he sprang up with his fists tightly clenched in fear. He knew it couldn't be Dad back already.

He didn't want to open the door. But certain kinds of people—like foreign witches—could get through doors even when you didn't open them. He peered through

the keyhole and could make out a dark coat like a cloak and, beyond it, the fairy lights still up at number 83. Didn't they know you have to take your decorations down by the 6th January? Jason thought he knew that coat. So, cautiously, he lifted the latch.

'Miss Wright!' he said in surprise. What on earth was she doing round here?

'Hello, Jason. Did you have a good time in Scotland?'

'Scotland?' said Jason, then remembered. 'Oh, that. No, we decided not to go to them relatives after all. We had an international Christmas here instead. For a change, you know.'

'Lovely idea,' Miss Wright nodded. 'I bet your Dad enjoyed that.'

She stood there clutching a large parcel and looking out of place.

'Yep,' said Jason. 'He did. I'm just waiting for him to get back from work now.'

'Then I won't keep you. I just wanted to wish you Happy New Year and *Buon Anno*.' And she leaned forward, thrust her parcel into Jason's hands and gave him a quick, clumsy hug.

Jason was too surprised even to say goodbye. He just stared after her as she scurried away in her flappy raincoat and disappeared down the stairway. He went back into the flat.

The parcel was wrapped in gold paper. It had the shape and the rattle of a tin of toffees. Or maybe it was chocolate biscuits? Or could it be nuts and raisins?

Jason wouldn't open it till Dad was back too. He wouldn't be long now. He wondered how had Miss Wright known where he lived? How had she known that a person never got too old for surprises? But then, Miss Wright knew everything.

Jason realized he was quite looking forward to school. Even if he had to sit next to Deirdre.

# Baboushka

Traditional, retold by

ROBERT SCOTT

Three men travelled together through a strange land.
For days they had moved steadily towards a distant star,
but now snow fell wetly from a dark, grey sky. They
would rest if they could find shelter rather than lose
their way completely.

It was Baboushka's house they came to.

She welcomed them in, built up the fire to dry their clothes, heated some soup to ease their hunger, shook out the mattresses for them to rest on.

Had they come a long way? They must be very tired. Where were they going? It must be very important to bring them such a distance at this time of the year.

'A star?' said Baboushka. 'You mean all you're doing is chasing after a star! In this weather? What on earth for?'

Patiently they explained. They weren't trying to reach a star, but this particular star was guiding them. They didn't know where they were going, but they would know when they arrived. There would be a baby.

'There are babies in the village,' said Baboushka. 'Stars, too, for that matter, when the skies are clear.'

No, she hadn't noticed a particularly bright star in the east.

They explained about the baby. He would be a prince, but one whose kingdom was the whole world, a saviour who would free people from their sins, who would bring peace. They were sure he was coming. They had gifts for him, gifts fit for such a prince.

'Why don't you come with us?' they asked.

'Me?' said Baboushka.

'Yes. You'll want to see him, won't you? He will be your king as well as ours.'

'But I don't have anything to take.'

'The only thing you need to bring is yourself.'

161

'But . . .' said Baboushka. 'But you can't travel now. It's snowing and you've lost your way.'

'The snow is passing. We shall push on as soon as we can see the star.'

'Perhaps tomorrow,' said Baboushka.

The snow cleared and the travellers were ready to leave well before dawn.

'You should come with us,' they said.

'I can't leave just like that,' said Baboushka. 'There's too much to do. I'll catch you up.'

When the men had gone Baboushka cleaned her pans and dishes, she raked out the fire and put away the mattresses, she fed and watered the animals. Then she tidied and dusted, swept and polished, picked up and put away until she was hungry.

'Frankincense,' she muttered as she broke herself some bread. 'Myrrh. Gold. I don't care if he is going to be a king, what use are such things to a child?'

So she searched through her cupboards and boxes until she found an old rattle and a coloured ball. She sorted out some material and made a rag doll. She took out a carved, wooden donkey she had loved ever since she had been a child herself.

'That's more like it,' she said, packing them into a sack.

Then she baked some bread, cut some dried meat, brought in a pitcher of water.

She washed and dusted and tidied up.

She took her goat to one neighbour to look after and her birds to another.

By the time she had finished, she was cold and hungry and tired. And it was snowing.

'Tomorrow,' she said.

She started up the fire again and made herself some soup.

When Baboushka started out the next day, there was no star to guide her and no tracks in the fresh snow.

'Oh dear,' she said. 'I should have gone when they asked me, but I couldn't. I couldn't just go and leave everything!'

She asked everyone she met, called at all the houses she came to.

'Three men? No, sorry. You're the first person we've seen in days.'

'A *star*! Well, there are lots of stars. No, nothing unusual about them.'

'A baby prince, you say? No, I'm afraid you've got the wrong place.'

'No.'

'No.'

'No.'

'But I *couldn't* just get up and leave,' said Baboushka. 'I just couldn't.'

So Baboushka went from place to place, looking for the new-born baby. And every year, when the time of the three strangers comes round, still she stops at the houses where there are children and leaves each of them a gift. 'If I can't give anything to the right baby,' she says, 'at least I can make some other children happy.' But, of course, each present she leaves is a gift to the baby she looks for, as well as to the child who receives it.

## Acknowledgements

The following stories were specially commissioned for this anthology and are all reprinted by permission of the author unless otherwise stated.

Rachel Anderson, 'The Good Witch Befana' © 1990 Rachel Anderson. Nina Beachcroft, 'White Christmas' © 1990 Nina Beachcroft. Helen East, 'Jon and the Nine Yule Nisse' © 1990 Helen East. Adèle Geras, 'Gifts' © 1990 Adèle Geras. Reprinted by permission of Laura Cecil, Literary Agent. John Gordon, 'The Christmas Cake' © 1990 John Gordon. Reprinted by permission of A P Watt Ltd. Dennis Hamley, 'Washing Their Socks' © 1990 Dennis Hamley. Rachel Hands, 'Beginning Christmas' © 1990 Rachel Hands. Hazel Hutchins, 'Wil's Tail' © 1990 Hazel Hutchins. Sheila Lavelle, 'Snowy' © 1990 Sheila Lavelle. Geraldine McCaughrean, 'The Rebellious Plum Pudding' © 1990 Geraldine McCaughrean. Anne Merrick, 'Really, Truly, Reilly' © 1990 Anne Merrick. Robert Scott, 'The Cat on the Dovrefell' and 'Baboushka', both © 1990 Robert Scott. Marilyn Watts, 'The Christmas Surprise' © 1990 Marilyn Watts. Duncan Williamson, 'The Robin and the Christmas Tree' © 1990 Duncan Williamson.

The editor and publisher are grateful for permission to include the following copyright material in this volume. Paul Biegel, 'Father Christmas's Clothes', trans. Patricia Crampton. Copyright Paul Biegel, Patricia Crampton and Glover & Blair Ltd. Katherine Gibson, 'Christmas through a Knothole' reprinted from *A Christmas Acorn* ed. Margaret Hainson (Bodley Head 1963) © Mr Lynton Wicks Pierce. Joel Chandler Harris, *Brer Rabbit's Christmas* retold by Nora Clarke, reprinted from *The Kingfisher Christmas Book* © Kingfisher Books Ltd 1985, by permission of Kingfisher Books Ltd. Alf Prøysen, 'Anderson the Carpenter and Father Christmas', trans. Patricia Crampton & Marianne Helweg, reprinted from *Stories for Christmas* by Alf Prøysen (1987). Reprinted by permission of Century Hutchinson Limited.

Illustrations are by: Jill Barton (Snowy); Michael Beach (Christmas through a Knothole); Michael Charlton (Father Christmas's Clothes); Bob Dewar (Brer Rabbit's Christmas *and* Baboushka); Peet Ellison (Jon and the Nine Yule Nisse); Annabel Large (The Christmas Surprise); Alan Marks (The Good Witch Befana); Pat Moffet (Gifts); Tony Morris (Really, Truly, Reilly); Claire Pound (Washing their Socks); Liz Roberts (Wil's Tail); Kate Rogers (White Christmas); Rachel Ross (The Christmas Cake); Susan Scott (The Christmas Story spreads: Mary and the Angel, The Journey, The Shepherds, The Birth, The Kings); Joseph Sharples (The Rebellious Plum Pudding); Duncan Storr (The Cat on the Dovrefell); John Tennent (The Robin and the Christmas Tree); Stephen Wilkin (Anderson the Carpenter and Father Christmas); Jenny Williams (Beginning Christmas).

Cover illustration by: Anthony Lewis
Oxford University Press would like to wish all their contributors and readers a Very Happy Christmas.